THE RED RIBBON

SURYA TEJA

Made with ♥ on the Notion Press Platform
www.notionpress.com

To the girl I met more than half a decade ago,
To the friend who saw me,
Who liked simply being around,
To the woman I grew obsessed with, over time.
To the woman whose mother, unknowingly,
Created a beautiful piece of art—her.
To the one who noticed my descriptions,
The one who reads not all,
But just enough,
The dreams where she was the centre.

She was the beginning of it all.
Her noticing became my spark,
And that spark became this book
You're holding in your hands.

And though she's not beside me today,
I hope, somewhere, someday,
She finds this story...
And maybe,
Finds me again.

Contents

Foreword

Some stories are born from imagination.

Others are pulled from the cracks between sleep and wakefulness.

This book is the latter.

Each chapter you're about to read once lived in a dream, twisting, shifting, refusing to be forgotten.

They started as flashes, fragments I scribbled late at night.

Then, they returned.

Again and again.

Until the dreams bled into reality.

What you hold now is not just a story.

It's a vision I couldn't escape.

And now... neither can you.

Welcome Inside.

Preface

There was a village named Kurnool, quiet, remote, and weathered by time.

At its edge stood a mansion... vast, forgotten, and shrouded in secrets.

Locals passed by with heads low, whispers buried under silence.

They said nothing, but they remembered.

Because centuries ago, in the mansion's backyard,

A woman had died.

Not by accident.

Not by nature.

But by something... unnatural.

She was buried. Then forgotten.

But she never left.

Now, Four hundred years later,

The wind in Kurnool carries her name again.

And her story begins... once more.

1
The Snatch

————•♡•————

<u>Wednesday, 29th March 1929.</u>

The village lay silent under the pale morning sky, a faint drizzle of snowflakes dusting the rooftops. A little girl, no older than six, stepped out of her home, her small footprints vanishing almost instantly under the soft frost. She wandered, her breath forming small, ghostly clouds.

As she explored, her tiny feet led her toward a place she had never noticed before, a backyard hidden behind her house. It was a place long forbidden, untouched for over Four centuries. Generations before her had whispered about it, warning never to step beyond its boundaries. But she had never even known it existed.

A narrow, forgotten path wound through gnarled trees, leading her toward a wall of old, black, and grey-coloured stones, each the size of a football, stacked unevenly upon one another. The structure looked fragile yet untouched, as if time itself hesitated to bring it down. At its centre stood a tall, narrow wooden door, divided into five weathered sections from top to bottom. From left to right, small iron rods were fixed across the wood, holding the pieces together, a rusted framework keeping the decayed planks from collapsing into dust.

She didn't even touch the door.

It opened by itself, slowly, silently, as if it had been waiting, as if it recognised her.

As if it was welcoming her home.

She stepped in.

What met her wasn't a room, but an abandoned backyard garden, forgotten by centuries. Dust clung to the air, to the brittle leaves that curled like old letters, unread. The land was dry, cracked, drained of life, as though even the roots had given up long ago. Shrubs stood like stone sculptures, stiff and sorrowful. Yet something in the stillness felt sacred.

Scattered across the garden were small, irregular granite slabs, large enough for one careful step each, forming a broken path that wove through the ruin. She walked softly, as if afraid her presence might disturb the silence too harshly.

Then,

There she saw it.

Its windows shattered, its walls sagging under time's weight.

All except for one window.

Unlike the others, this window was spotless, its polished white frame gleaming against the decay, its rectangular shape standing out in eerie perfection. It looked untouched, as if freshly placed in a world that had long been left to rot. But what truly caught the little girl's eye were the seven warm-white iron grills, evenly spaced across the glass. And there, wrapped tightly around one of the bars, was a red ribbon, its deep, dark hue absorbing the light, making everything else around it seem lifeless in comparison.

The ribbon was neither bright nor glossy, it was deep, dark red, absorbing the light around it, making every other color appear dull and lifeless. It stretched through the window's bars, trailing into the darkness beyond. It should have been tattered with age, but it was pristine, smooth and untouched, as if time itself refused to touch it.

She took a step closer.

Then another.

Curiosity made her brain rot into the dark, seeping into her thoughts like ink in water. Children were drawn to colours that stood out, and at that moment, the world around her blurred into shades of gray, all except for the red ribbon.

She reached out.

Her fingers brushed against the ribbon.

A sudden shift rippled through the world around her. The air vibrated. The colours drained. The flowers that had just begun to bloom wilted instantly. The vines curled and cracked. The ground darkened as though the very life had been sucked away.

The window, the ribbon, everything, aged before her eyes.

Startled, she pulled her hand back. In a blink, everything returned to how it was. The garden was dead again, the air still, the ribbon untouched.

A strange glee filled her. Was this magic?

She giggled and reached out again. *Touch. Decay. Release. Normal.*

She did it again.

And again.

Fascinated, she played with it, oblivious to the invisible hands tightening around her reality.

Then, suddenly, she pressed harder, unintentionally.

The ribbon moved.

Slowly, it curled inward, rewinding itself into the darkened room like a serpent retreating to its nest.

Her hand followed.

She barely realized it, but her fingertips were now past the bars, beyond the window frame. Her small arm slid through, her palm brushing the inside air-thick, heavy, wrong.

And then, she saw it.

A reflection.

Not her own.

Inside the dimly lit room, there sat The Lady, facing away from the window. Her frail hands clutched a delicate teacup. She did not move. She did not stir. She simply sipped.

The Lady was wearing deep, dark red-a shade so rich that in the dimness, it seemed to consume all the light, drawing every ounce of attention to itself. Her blouse had half sleeves, revealing her thin, pale arms, and around her neck hung a red diamond locket. The gem caught the faintest flicker of light, glowing like a drop of blood suspended in time.

The teacup in her hands was pearl white, an antique piece with delicate carvings etched into its fragile surface. Despite its elegance, there was something unsettling about the way she held it,her fingers curled around it with an eerie stillness, her grip firm yet effortless. She balanced it with a saucer, its rim slightly chipped, as if it had been used far longer than it should have been.

The Little Girl couldn't see her face.But she could see the red ribbon.

One end was still tied to the window. The other? It wound around The Lady's right wrist, its fabric coiling like a serpent, and stretched across her left shoulder, cascading down her side like a sash of flowing blood. The ribbon was thick, heavy, its texture almost velvet-like, yet it held an unnatural stillness, as if it were not just fabric, but something more.

The Red Saree Lady spoke, her voice a deep, guttural growl, laced with a whisper that crawled and coiled.

"Well, hello dear. Would you like some tea over here?"

It carried a weight, an eerie stillness as if something unseen echoed beneath her words.

The Little Girl replied, soft and innocent, *"My mother says tea is bad for kids. But you can drink boiled milk!"* She spoke with a childlike certainty, oblivious to the eerie stillness creeping through the air.

The Lady responded without a word, slowly rising to her feet, the soft creak of aged bones echoing through the dim room. She glided into the adjoining room. Moments later, she returned, carrying a glass jar, its surface fogged and stained with time. Inside, it held a dark, powdery substance like it looked like crushed shadows, the remains of nightmares sifted through ancient fingers, that seemed to shift and pulse faintly, as though it were alive.

The Lady replied, her lips curling slightly, *"How about this cacao granular?"*

She held the glass jar in her right hand, while her left rested firmly on her waist. She gripped the jar from the bottom, where the worn glass barely concealed the sharp gleam of her red nail polish, the color deep, unsettling, like something that had lived too long in silence. Her body leaned slightly, taking support from an ancient, warm brown special wooden chair-its frame carved with age, its fabric faded to a dull memory of elegance. She rested on it with casual poise, a still figure against time, her posture striking a delicate tension between grace and menace. One leg crossed over the other, and with the jar glowing dimly in her grasp, it was as if she belonged to both this world and the forgotten one beyond the door.

From behind, the dim, warm light seeped through the cracks of the room, casting uneven shadows and making her red saree glow with a dangerous, almost predatory aura, the fabric appearing alive as it fluttered softly without wind.

The Little Girl replied with a sudden spark of joy lighting up her face, "*Yes, yes! Sure!*" Her eyes gleamed with excitement, completely enchanted by the thought, unaware of the growing darkness curling around the room.

The Lady gently tilted the jar, letting the dark powder flow smoothly into a teacup. Unlike the delicate ones she used earlier, this cup was noticeably bigger, almost as if it was meant just for the little girl. The powder dissolved slowly, swirling into the liquid like inky tendrils, turning the warm milk into something darker, thicker, and strangely inviting.

She stirred it calmly, never breaking eye contact, as if waiting for the Little Girl to accept it without question. She gently placed the cup on the red ribbon.

The Little Girl innocently asked, tilting her head slightly, "*I didn't brush my teeth. My mom said if I eat or drink without brushing, my teeth will be eaten by a cavity.*"

Her voice was sweet and genuine, carrying the naive worries only a child could have, completely unaware that the real danger was never about her teeth.

The Lady leaned closer, her smile curling unnaturally as she whispered in a chilling tone,

"**Har roj kiya toh cavity aati hai... lekin tu kabhi kabhi aise kare toh, masti hai.**"

("If you do it every day, you'll get cavities... but if you do it once in a while, it's just fun.")

Her voice softened at the word fun, but it carried a chilling twist, making it sound more like a trap than comfort.

The Lady calmly placed the glass of cacao milk onto the red ribbon and passed it on to near the window, letting it slide smoothly. To any ordinary eye, it would have seemed impossible, the ribbon, thin and delicate, should never have been able to carry the cup's weight. It swayed gently as it slid the cup toward the window, defying logic.

Anyone might have noticed the strangeness of it, the unnatural way the ribbon held firm, but the Little Girl didn't even blink. Enthralled and carefree, she eagerly grabbed the cup without a second thought.

Then, she giggled, her eyes sparkling with innocent excitement.

"Is it?" she said, with a tone of encouragement, as if she'd long wished for someone to say exactly those words.

Smiling widely, she seized the cup and finished the cacao granular milk in a single playful swing, not a single sip slipped past her lips, nor did she pause for even a heartbeat, treating it like the happiest game she ever played.

Little did she know, the game had just begun.

As the Little Girl placed the cup back onto the Red Ribbon, her right palm accidentally brushed against its surface. The ribbon twitched. A slow, deliberate shudder ran through its length, as if it had just tasted something new, something it had been waiting for.

Then, it tightened.

A force, unseen yet overwhelming, slithered up her arm. The taste of the Lady's strange flavors still lingered inside her, and now the ribbon recognized it. It responded. It claimed her.

Before she could scream, before she could even understand, she was falling.

Her body jerked forward as the glass jar gaped open, its hollow depths twisting into an impossible void. The world warped and shattered, the air thick with an invisible pull. A silent tsunami of shadows erupted from the jar, swallowing her whole. She was sucked inward, limbs folding, vanishing, dissolving as if she were never meant to exist outside of it.

Just an empty jar, resting on the ribbon. After the girl disappeared, only her blue slippers remained on the floor. And then, everything was still.

The woman stepped forward, lifting another jar-this one filled with the same cacao granular-milk-colored swirl, thick and slow-moving, as if it remembered the one before. She cradled it carefully in both hands, her fingers tense but reverent.

Turning away from the silence, she moved behind the ancient wooden special wooden chair, where a tall, timeworn almirah stood, its warm brown surface faded and scuffed with age, the grain of the wood curling like forgotten script. The glass on its front was transparent, though slightly fogged by time, and its sliding doors whispered on their old tracks as she opened it.

Inside, rows of similar jars lined the shelves-each with a subtle hue of milk or chocolate powder, each still and sealed. She placed the new jar beside them without a word, her reflection faintly visible in the glass.

It wasn't just her.

It never was.

The surroundings, once twisted and alive, settled back into place. The faded backyard, the silent air, the old wooden door-all as if nothing had happened. The Red Ribbon hung motionless, swaying slightly, as if exhausted from what it had just consumed.

Inside, the Lady took her final sip of tea. The cup trembled in her grasp, a quiet hum vibrating through the air. She placed it down with an eerie deliberation, her fingers lingering over its rim.

Then, she snapped her fingers.

Her left elbow rested lazily on the special wooden chair, the same one that had always been there, Ancient, waiting, watching. She lifted her left hand, her red-polished nails catching the dim glow. The snap wasn't ordinary. It wasn't the sharp click of two fingers meeting.

It came from all of them.

A single motion, yet the sound rippled from every joint, every knuckle, every fingertip, as if her entire hand had come alive. And then, her entire body twisted violently, contorting into a spiraling mass. The air howled, bending to he command. A cyclonic wave, dark, shadowed, roaring like a silent storm, erupted from within her.

It surged forward, swallowing her whole.

Like a Tsunami crashing upon itself, her form spiraled into the waiting cup, pulled by an invisible force. The tea's surface did not ripple, did not stir, only absorbed her into its depths, as if she had always belonged there.

The cup remained.

Still warm. Still untouched.

And in its reflection, a pair of small, terrified eyes blinked from inside.

She owned this world now.

The world inside the cup.

And there was no way out.

2
The Secrecy

<u>Wednesday, 29th March 1929.</u>

Morning 5:45 AM

The wind was still.

The backyard lay untouched, as if no child had ever stepped into it.

The red ribbon fluttered slightly in the morning air, light as breath, yet soaked in something more profound, heavier, ancient.

The window is still open

The teacups were gone.

The Lady's chair remained.

And in the silence that followed, the kind that didn't hum with life but pulsed with something unseen, time itself seemed to pause.

Far away, beyond the overgrown fields and frost-laced woods, past the crumbling mansion and into the humming heart of the city, the world moved as usual.

But something had changed.

Every morning, the little girl would walk around the mansion, enjoying the fresh breeze like a free bird. But today, she was nowhere to be seen. Her absence made the mansion feel quieter than usual, and even the daylight seemed to be searching for her.

Slowly, people in the village began to wake up with the sunrise and the clucking of hens. The sounds of domestic animals-cows mooing, goats bleating, filled the air as homes came to life one by one.

The Mansion's servants began calling out for her, their voices ringing through the corridors. At least the walls gave back a response through an echo, but she didn't. Slowly, among the waiters, the words passed on. A search for the little girl had begun.

They began their search from the little girl's bedroom, moving through the long hallway, past the guest rooms, into the dining hall, kitchen, and the wide open central living area. They checked the library, the attic, the cellar, the indoor garden, even the storage rooms, balconies, and the stable area where the domestic animals-cows, goats, and hens-were kept. Room by room, floor by floor, they searched until they reached the main gate.

But there was one place they hadn't looked.

The backyard.

All the waiters then gathered outside one particular room of the mansion-one that only a select few servants were ever allowed to enter. But in their growing worry and confusion, they forgot the rules. In their panic, they stepped into the forbidden space: the Mansion Owner's private suite.

He was in the attic, listening to the soft crackle of the FM Graham Radio, lost in its peaceful hum. The attic itself was ancient-its wooden beams darkened with time, creaking gently like a whisper from generations past. It wasn't just a room; it was a vault of memories, passed down from forefathers, heavy with history.

Seated proudly in a worn-out wooden chair, he had tucked a white pillow beneath him for seat adjustment, a small gesture of comfort amidst the old wood. He sat cross-legged, right leg resting over the left, embracing the stillness of his solitude. Dressed simply in a half-sleeve cut banyan, a muffled cigar rested between the fingers of one hand, nearly six inches long, with two already reduced to ash. He inhaled it slowly through his nose, eyes half-closed, savoring its presence as if tasting an old memory.

In his other hand, a cup of steaming chai nestled gently in his palm. Below, a loosely tied dhoti completed his calm, traditional look. The FM music softly echoed around the attic while the sunrise poured in through the high window, warm and golden, casting a beautiful glow that made the moment feel like a perfect, untouched scene from another time.

As the soft static of the FM Graham Radio continued to hum in the attic, the mansion's owner leaned back further into his wooden chair, shifting slightly to readjust the white pillow he had placed for comfort. The muffled crackle of the cigar in his right hand faded into the silence, and he took a slow, deep breath through his nose, savoring the burn of tobacco and the scent of chai in his left hand. His legs crossed, right over left, in practiced ease as he admired the golden wash of the sunrise flooding through the attic window.

To him, it was a morning of perfect peace.

Until he heard it.

The sound of hurried footsteps on the stairs—dozens of them. Voices layered over one another. His serenity cracked just slightly.

A hesitant knock echoed on the attic door.

The Man in the Chair turned his head toward the noise, his expression still unreadable. Then came his voice, deep, drawn out, heavy with age and weight.

A voice so resonant, even the walls of the mansion seemed to hold their breath in fear of its echo. In the suit room around him, large canvas paintings imported from Italy adorned the walls-masterful depictions of misty forests, storm-kissed coastlines, and moonlit meadows. Yet something about them felt... wrong. The brushstrokes, though exquisite, seemed to move when one wasn't looking. Behind him, a towering antique wall clock stood like a sentinel, its pendulum swinging slowly, each tick carving silence like a blade, counting not just seconds, but something older. Something waiting.

"*What... haaappenned...?*"

One of the Servant Responded

"*Sir...*" came a voice from the other side. "*You're... You're girl... she's missing.*"

He didn't move right away. Just one slow drag from the cigar, ash dropping soundlessly onto the floorboards.

Then, placing the cup of chai carefully onto the small table beside him, he finally exhaled.

The question stretched like smoke, curling into every corner of the attic, seeping down the stairs like a slow-moving storm. Silence lingered in the room like thick mist. No one dared to break it, not yet.

The old man leaned back, exhaling two... three slow puffs from his muffled cigar, each one rising like curling shadows. Then, with a flick of his wrist, he tossed the smoldering stub out through the fully opened attic window, no glass, no barrier, just the wind waiting to catch it. The ash trailed behind like a dying comet, vanishing into the light of day.

The silence stayed a moment longer, heavy as stone.

Just as the last ember of his cigar disappeared into the morning sky, the old man's hand shifted, not to rest, but to reach. From a small shelf beside his chair, he picked up a delicate antique jar, one laced with gold trim and hairline cracks, an heirloom, perhaps, or just another relic of rage.

With a sudden burst of fury, he hurled it, not at anyone in particular, but with enough force that it shattered against the wall just above the heads of the gathered servants. The sound cracked through the attic like thunder. Shards rained down like jagged hailstones, clinking across shoulders and the wooden floor. The servants flinched but didn't move, their fear anchoring them in place.

"I want my Daughter!!" he roared, his voice not just loud, but torn from the pit of a breaking soul. It wasn't just anger; it was grief clawing its way out, wrapped in fury, soaked in sorrow. The sound shook the walls, cracked the air, like something ancient and wounded finally breaking open. His chest heaved, his eyes blazing—not just with rage, but the unbearable ache of a father slipping into despair.

The servants stood frozen, clueless, rattled, some still crouched on the floor, quietly gathering the shattered remains of the antique jar.

The old man's eyes blazed as he rose slightly from his chair, voice thundering with command:

"Stop picking up those goddamn pieces!" he bellowed. *"Instead of sweeping up antiques, go find her! Search the entire village-every street, every corner!"*

He pointed angrily, breath heavy with fury and pain.

"I don't care if it's house, religion, or caste-tear through every wall if you must. Knock on every door, shout into every alley. Search every corner of this village, every hound, every shadow. Hunt through their homes, tear open their sheds-hell, even if

they're in their bloody, busy bathrooms, drag them out if they've seen anything! No matter what stands in your way, break it. Bring her back. Bring my daughter back!"

Then came the final blow-words heavy with weight:

"And tell them this..." he growled, voice sharp as a blade.

"Sitarama Raju Garu pampincharu ani cheppu!"

"(Sitarama Raju sent... us!!!!)"

The name dropped like thunder across the room. Every servant straightened. The air thickened. No one dared to disobey.

Everyone dispersed like trained soldiers under the command of a furious sergeant. Without wasting a second, they stormed out of the mansion and flooded into the village like a wave crashing ashore.

Before leaving, each servant grabbed a framed photograph of the little girl from the grand living room wall-dozens of portraits capturing her laughter, her stillness, her innocence. The mansion had no shortage of her pictures, and within moments, every single one of them had been taken. One photo per servant, clutched tightly like a sacred token, and with that, they left the mansion behind.

At first, they knocked-loud, urgent, desperate.

But when doors didn't open fast enough...

They didn't wait.

They thrust through them.

Wooden latches splintered, curtains tore, and startled families leapt from their beds as the servants barged into homes uninvited, shouting the same line over and over like a war cry:

"Sitarama Raju Garu pampincharu !!!!"

"(Sitarama Raju sent us!!!!)"

With the girl's picture held up like a warrant, they scanned the faces of villagers in every home.

One of the servants, breathless and wild-eyed, stepped forward and asked a trembling villager:

"Have you seen her? Sitarama Raju's daughter is missing... did you see anything?"

The village, once quiet in its morning routines, was now echoing with the thunder of searching footsteps and rising panic.

ᛈᛈᛈ

They kept searching until noon. Some of the servants, drained and hungry, returned to the mansion for lunch. Their faces were pale, voices gone. They couldn't even speak.

Sitarama Raju spotted them from the attic balcony. As he exhaled a thick puff of cigar smoke, his eyes burned with disbelief and rage. He stared at them, a storm brewing behind his gaze. Without a word, he removed the cigar from his mouth, struck it against the ground, and crushed it with his bare right foot, twisting and grinding it with both feet until nothing but ashes remained.

Then, with a furious breath, he turned and stormed into his suite.

There, from his antique drawer, he pulled out a beautiful, uniquely crafted diamond-shaped box. It rested on four tiny legs, sealed with a lock. Next to it lay a rectangular box, already open, inside which was a set of cigars.

Sitarama Raju reached for the locket around his neck, shaped like a tiger's claw. As he held it, a sudden memory struck him, he had hidden the diamond box's key inside the sacred thread (Aranjanam) tied around his waist. With a swift motion, he pulled the thread with his left hand, unhooked the key with his right, and unlocked the box.

Inside: Wall gun bullets.

As the lid creaked open, a faint glint of metal greeted his eyes. For a moment, he didn't move. Just stared.

Then, slowly, his lips curled, not entirely, just to the left. A cold, cunning smile. The kind that had haunted enemies in older wars. A smile that meant something dark was about to follow. A signature expression he wore when he knew that some innocents might suffer, but it no longer mattered, not when it came to his daughter.

He reached in, his hand shaking, not from fear, but rage, grabbing a handful of the wall gun bullets.

But surprisingly, there was no dust.

The bullets were clean. Immaculate. As if they'd just been forged.

Because the diamond-shaped box wasn't just for show, it was crafted with a rare precision, an airtight seal so strong, not even air dared to enter. Decades had passed, yet not a speck of time had touched what lay inside.

This box wasn't just a container. It was a vault of vengeance, waiting for the day it would be opened.

Sitarama Raju stared at the bullets resting in his palm-perfect, silent, deadly. His eyes burned as he tightened his grip and then flung them forcefully onto the table before him.

Clack! Clink! Clatter!

The sound rang through the attic like war drums. The bullets scattered, some rolling to the edges, one clinking off the wooden floor before skidding to a stop near a pair of black boots.

It belonged to a man-tall, six feet, charming with a sharp jawline and a grin that always carried a hint of mischief. He wore a crisp white shirt, sleeves slightly rolled up, paired with black jeans, and carried a dark leather jacket slung over his shoulder. A Hanuman locket swung gently from his neck, catching a ray of sunlight like a divine spark. On his wrist, an antique watch ticked steadily, a gift from the very same attic decades ago.

He bent down slowly, picked up the bullet between his fingers with a smirk, and chuckled. It was him. Sitarama Raju's younger brother.

"I found the bullet... but where's the machine to load it?" Abhimanyu teased, his voice calm, laced with quiet tension.

He flipped the bullet once in his hand, letting it catch the light, then looked up at his elder brother with a playful glint in his eyes, part mischief, part challenge.

Still holding the bullet out like a silent question, he began walking toward his elder brother.

Each step echoed in the old suite room—

Taap... Taap... Taap...

The sound of his black boots slicing through the heavy silence, announcing his presence with every click on the wooden floor.

In the meantime, Sitaramaraju reached for the gun.

He retrieved the wall-mounted gun.—hung there for years, a relic of the past more honoured than used. He pulled it from its mount with a yank that stirred dust from the wall. For decades, it had been cleaned only for festivals or ceremonies-never used. But this day was different. Today, it was war.

He came and sat near the table, sinking into the creaky, old attic chair with a heavy sigh. He flipped the loading chamber open, the metal creaking slightly under his touch, and began to load just two bullets.

His breath deepened. Each movement is deliberate.

One bullet slid in with purpose.

Second bullet... sealed with rage.

Then, locking it shut with a swift snap, he stood still for a moment, holding the weapon down by his side.

Suddenly, Sitaramaraju heard his brother's footsteps, coming from his back, the soft yet deliberate thud of black boots pressing against the wooden floor. But Sitarama Raju didn't even turn back. His focus remained on the task at hand, loading the gun with a calmness that contrasted with the fury boiling within him.

On his way out, he grabbed an old microphone connected to a speaker system, once used for announcements across the mansion grounds.

His brother followed him, patiently watching his every move. There was no rush in his steps. Marching to the balcony, he looked down at the stunned servants. Without hesitation, he aimed.

Bang!

The shot echoed through the valley like a warning carved into thunder.

Then, gripping the rusted iron of the old microphone, his voice crackled to life—low, sharp, and laced with fury. *"How dare you return to the mansion without my daughter?"*

He fired a bullet straight into one servant's right shoulder-his aim was deliberate. Not the heart. Not a kill. Just enough to disable-enough pain to remind them that their job wasn't done until his daughter was found. He wanted their legs and hands to still function-for the search to go on.

Sitarama Raju's eyes didn't blink. The misfire had only stoked the fire inside him-rage now spilling out in waves. He turned toward the other servants with a snarl, his voice thunderous:

"She's not here! Something else is going on! Keep searching! Don't leave a single house unchecked!"

Suddenly, the injured servant's body twitched, and he coughed blood through clenched teeth. His voice, weak but thick with fear, broke through the tension:

The servant screamed and collapsed, clutching his shoulder in agony. But his agony was swallowed in the chaos of the market's rush. He collapsed to the ground, writhing, his right hand clutching his left shoulder, trying in vain to squeeze out the pain or forget it, even for a breath.

Local people around the mansion started shouting in terror, scattering in all directions—running up here and there but always away from the mansion. Mothers grabbed children. Market carts were overturned. The air filled with chaos and dust, as if the mansion itself had erupted in violence.

A vegetable vendor paused mid-shout, torn between fleeing and helping, but one look at the mansion's arch sent him running, leaving behind his cart, his courage, and the bleeding man who now lay in a spreading pool of dust and fear.

From the balcony, Sitarama Raju stood still, smoke curling from the barrel of his gun like a warning.

And then... his brother spoke, standing beside him, arms crossed with that same amused smirk-tilted his head and said,

"No, big brother... You should always aim for the HEAD"

His tone was playful, but his eyes gleamed with something sharper. A dangerous glint of mischief... maybe even madness.

Before Sitaramaraju could respond, Abhimanyu reached out and snatched the wall gun from his elder's hands with a swift, smooth motion.

With a cocky breath, he scanned the servants frantically scrambling in the courtyard below. His gaze locked on one of them-a lanky man with a mop of wild, overgrown hair that looked like grass left uncut in monsoon.

"That one looks like a bush," he muttered with a chuckle, aiming.

But just as he was about to fire—

Sitaramaraju grabbed the barrel and yanked it to the side with sudden force, his voice rising with an anger so cold it burned:

"I need them."(Wasn't going to Trigger)

Abhimanyu's finger still squeezed the trigger.

BOOM!

The bullet flew—

not into flesh, but into a large metal drum by the mansion's archway.

The drum exploded. Water blasted out like a small flood, crashing over the cobblestone and washing across the feet of the mansion gates.

The sound was deafening. But unlike the first shot, this time there were no villagers screaming nearby.

They had already run far from the scene.

And yet

You could still hear the echoes.

The cries of dogs, the rustling of birds flying from trees, and somewhere in the shadowed corners of the mansion, the frantic hooves of a horse kicking against its stable.

Silence. Then-Chaos.

The village had frozen.

Every corner, every stall, every home held its breath.

Those few brave enough to look back toward the mansion saw not a home, but a WAR ZONE from now.

And above all that stood the two brothers-one calm and teasing, the other furious and unbreakable—together, yet on the edge of something darker.

And still

The girl was missing.

ᐅᐅᐅ

Even as chaos simmered in the air, Sitarama Raju stood unmoved, his blood boiling, his eyes scanning every soul like a predator cornered. Trust had withered. Faith in the people under his roof? Gone.

He didn't speak it, but it was written in the way he clenched the barrel of his gun, the way his left eye twitched ever so slightly.

He didn't believe anyone anymore, not even the ones who had served him for decades.

Then,

A voice cracked the silence.

"Sir! Sir!"

One of the servants shouted, stumbling forward, breath heaving. The same one with the overgrown hair—scared, sweating, and still alive by a hair's breadth.

"The one you shot... he knows something about your daughter!"

The room froze.

Even Sitaramaju Raju blinked-just once.

Abhimanyu, still standing behind, chuckled darkly. He adjusted the Hanuman locket hanging from his neck, his voice soaked in cold satisfaction.

He walked up beside his elder brother, whispered with a sly grin:

"Good... you stopped just in time. Sometimes, mercy pays off... as if we knew something deeper was going on."

Abhimanyu Shouts From the Balcony

"It's good, My Brother left him without killing him."

Sitarama Raju didn't respond. He was already on the move-gun in hand, rage in his stride, heading back to the servant bleeding on the floor, now unconscious. But not for long.

Because now... he wanted answers.

Real ones.

Or he was going to dig them out-piece by piece.

Sitarama Raju didn't wait.

He marched straight down the stairs, his face hard, eyes blazing, as he closed in on the servant bleeding out on the cold stone floor. His voice cut through the silence like a blade.

"Tell me what you have... too ?"

He growled, crouching beside the wounded man.

The servant writhed, half-conscious, gripping his shoulder, his breath short and ragged.

Just then, Abhimanyu stepped in, calm but swift-his boots clicking sharply behind him. He tossed the First-Aid Kit down beside his elder brother with a nod.

Inside it, among the gauze, antiseptics, and sutures, lay a worn, cold instrument gleaming in the dim light: the bullet extractor, also known as a surgical forceps or bullet clamp.

His brother raised an eyebrow.

"You shoot them, I patch them... what a team."

Sitarama Raju didn't smile.

He leaned in close-his breath heavy, eyes wild with a storm of anxiety and fury.

The bullet extractor clinked softly in his gloved hand, the metal cold, unforgiving.

The servant's eyes fluttered open, lips trembling as he coughed up pain.

Sitarama Raju pressed the extractor just above the wound, not yet digging, just close enough to threaten.

"Answer now... what you know," he hissed, his voice low, trembling with suppressed rage.

"Otherwise, I'm gonna stake it straight into your heart this time."

His grip tightened.

Because now...

He needed answers.

Real ones.

Or he was going to dig them out, piece by piece.

His grip tightened.

His brother stood behind him, silent now-his gaze sharp, reading every flicker of truth or deception on the servant's pale face.

A single bead of sweat rolled down the servant's temple.

Then, barely above a whisper...

"Master... It's not in the mansion, Master..."

His body convulsed.

He gasped.

And then, he fainted.

Sitarama Raju didn't flinch. He turned to the others, voice cutting like a blade:

"Bring the country liquor!"

The command struck like thunder.

The servants hesitated, shocked, confused-until one of them finally moved. A few moments later, he returned, holding a tall glass bottle wrapped at the neck with coarse brown jute rope.

It looked old—almost sacred.

A rural artifact of tradition and necessity.

The milky liquor inside glowed faintly in the dim mansion light. The bottle stood heavy, sturdy, with the rope coiled tightly around its neck like a noose of silence. Its surface still held the moisture of cool storage, like something kept hidden for moments of truth.

Everyone was now standing ankle-deep in the thick, wet mud, splattered across the ground after the second bullet had struck the old iron drum near the mansion arch, bursting it open and flooding the path. The area beneath the arch was soaked, a messy mixture of slush and grit. The wounded servant, too, lay drenched, his body caked with sticky mud, the grainy earth clinging to his skin, mixing with the blood that still pulsed slowly from his shoulder, creating a disturbing swirl of red and brown down his veins.

The servant came rushing back with the Sāra bottle, but before he could hand it over, Sitarama Raju snatched it from his grip, and the liquid inside shuddered within the glass from the force.

And with a sudden feral rage, he bit the cork off with his teeth, like a wild animal snapping bone.

He lifted the fainted servant's head and poured the sharp, pungent Sāra into his mouth.

The effect was instant.

The man coughed violently, spasming back to life. The liquor spilled down his chin, soaking his torn shirt.

For a fleeting second, he stared at the mess, confused, almost thinking it was just cheap wine.

But then he remembered.

He had been shot.

By the very man who now held him.

And was feeding him liquor with the same hands that once aimed a gun.

There was something poetic and cruel in it.

So he drank.

Not just from the bottle, but from the moment.

Drank like it was survival.

Drank until the bottle was half-empty.

And then, Abhimanyu snatched the bottle away.

"That's enough for the day," he said coldly.

Then, stepping closer, eyes narrowing, voice shifting from stern to cruel playfulness:

"Talk... (Extending the Word),

Or this bottle becomes the first toast of your death day—

And trust me, it'll be today."

After Abhimanyu's chilling threat, the injured servant wiped his mouth with his trembling hand, coughed out the bitterness, and swallowed whatever wine still lingered.

He blinked through the sting and finally spoke—

"It's... It's the Sadhu," he said hoarsely.

Sitarama Raju, who had already turned halfway, froze.

"Huh?" His voice was sharp, suspicious. He spun fully now, facing the crowd.

"Is there anyone here who knows a man named Sadhu?" he barked.

"Find him. Bring him to me alive.

My daughter... she will be with him. I know it."

But just then, the bloodied servant tapped his chest with his dirtied fingers, as if summoning strength from his very soul.

"No... Master, The Sadhu. Not a Sadhu..."

Sitarama Raju's jaw clenched. His patience thinned like thread under fire.

With rising irritation, he snapped,

"Did I shoot your shoulder or your sense of direction?. You uneducated moron, speak completely!"

The servant winced but gathered his breath.

"No, Master... The Sadhu, the one who lives near the old temple... the one no one visits after dark."

Sitarama Raju's jaw clenched. His voice was tightly controlled, simmering just beneath the surface.

"So you're saying... the Sadhu took my daughter?"

Each word pressed through his teeth like a loaded trigger.

The servant coughed, wet, heavy, his body trembling under the pain.

"No, Master... he didn't take her..."

He gasped, struggling for breath, eyes flickering between fear and urgency.

"But... he said, he saw the girl... before she even vanished."

Sitarama Raju's face stiffened.

The words "he saw the girl" echoed like a curse blown through a hollow cave.

"He said what...?"

Sitarama Raju's voice cut through the air like a blade, sharp, low, disbelieving. Not a question... a warning.

As if daring the servant to repeat something that shouldn't be true.

But the servant coughed, his breath shallow and uneven.

Fear mixed with pain made his words tremble.

"I... I didn't believe him, Master," he stammered. *"He just said it so calmly... like he already knew... like he saw her..."*

Sitarama Raju's jaw clenched. His face froze, jaw tight. The look he gave the servant wasn't anger, it was precision, the kind of gaze a hunter gives before letting the arrow fly.

But the servant coughed again, his breath shallow. Fear mixed with pain made his words tremble.

"He... he said the girl was chosen. That her soul has

The scent (exaggerating)... the scent of the other world, Master..."

A cold silence fell.

Sitarama Raju stood up slowly, the weight of those words sinking in. His jaw clenched. His fingers twitched near the trigger of the gun again.

"Call the villagers. Bring every man with a lantern. We ride to the temple..."

He looked at Abhimanyu, sharp, still as a blade beside him.

"Tonight."

Before Sitarama Raju could finish commanding the others to take him to the hospital, a few servants rushed forward, ready to lift the wounded man. But Sitarama Raju raised his hand, halting them mid-step.

He looked down at the bloodied servant, whose body trembled more from fear than pain, and asked with a low, almost curious voice,

"What's your name?"

The servant, weak but conscious, looked up and replied, *"My Name is Giri... Master."*

Sitarama Raju nodded once, his fierce expression softening into something nobler, almost fatherly. With a hint of pride and a rare curve of a smile, he said:

"Then you, Giri... your family will be taken care of by us for the rest of your life. And as for your drink, every weekend, you'll receive an old bottle from my wine cellar. I don't want you drinking every day."

The crowd wasn't silent.

They were shocked, eyes widened, mouths slightly parted. No one had expected such generosity. Whispers began to stir among the villagers and servants alike. A few faces, clearly etched with jealousy, didn't hide it well. Brows tightened, jaws clenched.

Loyalty had just earned Giri a fortune, and now, some were wandering like hungry dogs, sniffing for the next bit of information that might buy their own salvation.

Others stood silent, as if a bullet had just entered their heart.

Not from a gun-but from the weight of a truth they should've spoken, but didn't.

ᐅᐅᐅ

Abhimanyu walked beside him-silent, alert, and carrying the weight of unspoken questions.
Meanwhile, Sitarama Raju had dismissed most of his servants, retaining only a select few, along with trusted village heads and ward members. With no need for horses, they walked between two walls-the crumbling side of an old house to the right and the moss-covered backyard wall of the mansion to the left. Their path was narrow, silent, and stretched into shadow.
A path long forgotten, swallowed by overgrown grass and creeping roots.

They had never cared about this backyard.
It was a forgotten realm, left to grow wild. Beside the old backyard door-rusted at the hinges and half-swallowed by vines-the gnarled roots of the mansion had begun to rise from the earth like the bones of a sleeping giant. Cracks lined the lower walls, where time had crept in, unnoticed.

At the far end of that backyard, shrouded in mystery and shadow, stood the ancient temple. Despite the hour still lingering in daylight, the temple remained draped in darkness, as if the sun itself refused to touch it. The air grew colder the closer they stepped, and the scent of damp stone and moss filled their lungs.

Sitarama Raju led the group in silence, his boots crunching on twigs and wet mud, the long rifle slung over his shoulder like a silent threat. His figure cut a grim silhouette against the fading sky-still, sharp, and brooding.

They walked along an old, rarely used path, almost taken back by the forest. As they moved ahead, they saw the ancient temple to their right, its dark shape surrounded by thick banyan trees. On their left was the backyard of the mansion, partly visible through the bushes, just 300 meters between them, but it felt like they belonged to two completely different worlds.

Torches were lit as the trees thickened, their flames jittering with every gust of wind. The air grew heavier, more silent, as if it too held its breath. Shadows danced across the cracked stone pathway that veered slightly toward the temple, each flicker painting twisted shapes onto the ground.

Every footstep echoed, not against stone or soil, but against memory, unspoken fears and half-told stories buried beneath the tangled roots.

No horses. No wheels. No grand entrance.

Only footsteps.

Only whispers.

Only the sound of truth closing in on something long hidden, between the backyard's last fence post and the temple's crumbling threshold.

The temple stood in a twilight of its own, resting in darkness even under the bright sun. Shadows twisted like roots, bleeding through the cracks of ancient stone. Banyan trees covered every corner, their tangled arms gripping the structure like guardians of something forbidden.

At the entrance gateway tower, two massive banyans had merged into one, forming an accidental arch of nature, yet it felt anything but accidental.

And there, high on that arch, sat the Sadhu.

Cross-legged. Motionless. A wooden staff upright in front of him, his left palm resting gently on its head. His matted hair draped like coiled ropes over his shoulders. Ash smeared across his chest. He looked less like a man and more like an echo carved from silence.

As the villagers stood frozen, breath caught in their throats and eyes locked on the eerie figure above...

The Sadhu tilted his head slightly, his messy hair swaying gently with the breeze. A faint, eerie smile appeared on his face.

Then, with a soft chuckle that echoed unnaturally in the silence, he said, with his eyes still closed.

"You haven't found even an inch of a clue about your girl." His laughter followed—quiet, measured... as if he knew something no one else did.

Sitarama Raju's anger erupted like a storm held too long. His breath grew sharp, chest rising with fury, and the servants instinctively moved to seize the Sadhu, but with a swift glance and a subtle motion, he stopped them.

Sitarama Raju raised his hand and gently waved his middle and index fingers together, a silent signal they all knew well.

It meant: *Hold. Not yet*

The air around him crackled with restrained rage, but his eyes never left the Sadhu.

Sitarama Raju stepped forward, his voice low but firm, laced with the weight of suspicion.

"My people said you claimed... that you saw my daughter before she vanished," he said, eyes narrowed, studying the Sadhu's every breath.

The Sadhu didn't flinch. His eyes remained closed, as if the question was merely a ripple on a still pond.

The Sadhu's head barely moved, but his voice, calm as flowing water, answered plainly,

"Yes, I did."

Sitarama Raju's nostrils flared. He turned his face to the side, exhaled sharply, blowing out the storm rising within him. Then, in a tone biting but measured, he said,

"Well... where is she now?"

The Sadhu's reply came like a whisper caught in the wind,

"She is in the future."

Sitarama Raju blinked. A pause. His jaw tightened as confusion twisted with rage. Again, he turned to the side, exhaling with effort, fists clenched, and spoke-

"I can't understand, Sadhu... can you please enlighten us?"

His tone tried to stay calm, but each word felt like a nail held back from piercing the wood. He blew out another breath through his teeth.

The Sadhu's eyes opened slowly, glowing, almost reflective, like ancient embers flickering to life.

As his gaze lifted toward Sitarama Raju, the very trenches of the banyan tree seemed to stir. Roots coiled tighter, leaves rustled without wind, and for a moment, it felt as if the entire tree had saddled up behind him-alive, listening.

With a sharp, cutting look that sliced through the tension, the Sadhu spoke,

"Didn't you're grandparents ever tell you the stories...About **The Red Ribbon Girl?"**

Sitarama Raju replied with a steady nod, his voice lower now, touched by something between memory and unease.

"Yes... I heard. I grew up listening to those stories."

The Sadhu, still seated calmly atop the banyan arch, leaned forward ever so slightly and asked in a gentler tone,

"What did you hear about her, then?"

Sitarama Raju took a breath, glancing sideways as if searching the air for pieces of an old tale.

"The same old stuff," he said quietly.

"She appears when a girl is about to begin her first blood..."

He continued, *"For generations, they passed her story down. But... my grandparents never told me her name."*

His eyes slowly lifted to the Sadhu again, now filled with curiosity as much as caution.

"Do you know her name?" he asked, his voice almost a whisper.

The Sadhu responded, his voice like dried leaves brushing stone,

"Yes... I know her name. But I won't spill it out in front of Abhimanyu, you're still shielding behind him."

Sitarama Raju didn't speak a word. His expression tightened, and with just a sharp glance—no more than a shift in his piercing gaze, he signaled.

Immediately, the younger servants and villagers began stepping back, understanding the silent command. Their footsteps faded into the shadows, leaving only the elder ward members and village heads behind, men of Sitarama Raju's age and time.

Just as Abhimanyu was about to turn and follow the others, the Sadhu, still seated cross-legged atop the natural arch, raised his hand slightly and spoke:

"You... stay back."

The Abhimanyu froze mid-step, startled, and turned around slowly, his face caught between obedience and uncertainty. The air grew still again, the banyan branches above rustling like whispers trying to listen.

Abhimanyu raised both hands in the air, gesturing silently toward Sitarama Raju, his brows furrowed in confusion. With a hushed voice, barely more than a breath, he mouthed:

"Why me?"

But before Sitarama Raju could respond, the Sadhu, still seated like stone atop the banyan arch, turned his head slightly. As if the shadows themselves had carried the question through the rustling leaves and into his ears, he replied—his voice calm, knowing, and strangely distant:

"Well... eventually, with time, you'll come to know everything."

With that, he gently raised his wooden staff and pointed it toward Abhimanyu—not threateningly, but like a teacher marking a destined pupil.

The moment stilled.

Even the wind seemed to pause.

Abhimanyu stepped forward quietly, coming to stand beside Sitarama Raju. He leaned casually against a tree stem, one leg crossed over the other, trying to match the composure of his elder, but the weight of the moment still clung to his shoulders.

Sitarama Raju's eyes narrowed. His patience, already stretched thin, began to splinter.

He took a step forward, voice low but firm:

"What's her name then?"

The Sadhu didn't move. Instead, he closed his eyes again, as though even the question brushed against forbidden truths.

"I can't say her name," he murmured, voice like wind rustling through bone-dry leaves.

"Not here... not anywhere. But I can tell you where she is."

That was when Sitarama Raju's memory snapped like a taut string.

His voice cracked, not with weakness, but rage-fueled urgency:

"Okay, wait-why do I have to know about her?"

He clenched his fists, stepping forward again.

"I didn't come here for legends or riddles... I came to ask you—

You said you saw my daughter...

WHERE. DID. YOU. SEE. HER. GO? ".

ᏐᏐᏐ

The silence that followed wasn't empty.

It was heavy.

The Sadhu, eyes still closed, didn't hesitate. His voice was calm, yet it struck like thunder:

"If you want your daughter back, then you must know the story of the Red Ribbon Girl... because she... she is the one who might have taken her."

And just like that, A sudden gust tore through the temple grounds.

The wind howled.

Everyone's clothes flapped violently, torches flickered, and dry leaves swirled like ghosts in a circle. The banyan trees creaked and moaned as if whispering forgotten things. The wind wasn't cold, but it carried something... unnatural.

Abhimanyu flinched, instinctively pulling his shawl closer. He looked around, confused and unnerved.

"Where is this wind even coming from?,

This temple's abandoned... closed from all sides... yet this wind feels alive," he thought.

Sitarama Raju stood frozen, then his knees gave way.

He sank to the ground, his hands gripping the dust below, chest heaving.

A storm brewed inside his mind.

"Are the stories real? Did she really take my daughter? Why... Why her?"
His thoughts spiraled like the wind around him.
"Is this a bloodline sin? Is this curse buried in my veins?"
He trembled.
"She's only two years away... Two years from her first blood... How would the Ribbon Girl know that?"
And with that thought, a hundred more came crashing in.

Sitarama Raju stared at the earth beneath him, as if answers might rise from the soil.

But all he could hear was the growling wind and the unspoken name that echoed in silence.

Sitarama Raju collapsed to his knees, his sobs echoing through the temple ruins like shattered prayers. His cries weren't just of pain; they were of a father torn between belief and desperation.

Abhimanyu, who had been silently standing nearby, finally moved closer. Gently, he placed a hand on Sitarama Raju's shoulder, trying to anchor him through the storm inside. The village heads, from a distance, stunned by the look of Sitaramaraju, slowly approached as well. They had never seen Sitarama Raju cry, not for war, not for loss-but now, for his daughter, he wept like the world had ended.

The torches flickered harder. The wind howled through the banyan branches above. Yet the Sadhu didn't flinch. Not a breath of emotion passed his ash-streaked face. His wooden staff stood as still as he did.

Finally, the Sadhu spoke-his voice dry, heavy like dust from another century.

"I cannot speak her name," he said, eyes still closed. *"I cannot even whisper it... because she was never born as you and I were.*
She is born of rage.

Of silence.

Of things your kind forgot to fear."

The crowd went dead still.

"But…" he continued, "*I can help you with two things.*"

Hearing this, Sitarama Raju wiped his eyes with his forearm, pushing away the curtain of tears that blurred his sight. With trembling limbs, he crawled forward and bowed on his knees below the Sadhu's perch, his voice hoarse with grief.

"*What are they?*" he asked. "*What are the two things?*"

The Sadhu's voice curled through the wind like a chant lost in time.

"*There are two things I can tell you,*" he said, still unmoving, still serene-as if what he was about to say weighed more than the wind itself.

Sitarama Raju's tear-soaked face tilted up, clinging to those words with a desperate hope.

"*One,*" the Sadhu said, "*I saw your daughter… walking toward the backyard of your mansion. Alone. Unafraid. As if she were being called.*"

Gasps escaped a few lips behind him. Abhimanyu's eyes widened.

Sitarama Raju's mouth opened in disbelief. "*But we searched every….*"

"*Not where you should have,*" the Sadhu interrupted.

He paused, letting the silence hang.

"*And the second…*" His tone darkened, deeper now. "*There is an old witch… far beyond your village. Across the shadowed ridges, past the dry riverbed. She lives alone.*"

"*She?*" Sitarama Raju whispered, still kneeling.

"*Yes,*" the Sadhu nodded slightly, eyes half-lidded. "*She is not like others. She has meditated for decades and trained under storms, under eclipses, under blood moons. Her power is ancient, drawn from the veins of time itself. She is the only one in this entire land... who might know how to reach the girl with the red ribbon."*

He leaned slightly forward now, his voice sharp.

"But beware... she doesn't give answers without a price. And she never lies."

After a moment of shared silence, Sitarama Raju and the Abhimanyu slowly stood up, bowing respectfully toward the Sadhu. They offered their gratitude with folded hands before turning away, the air still thick with the remnants of their desperate plea.

As they descended from the temple archway, Sitarama Raju called over a few of his most trusted servants.

"Bring food... fresh fruits... whatever we have. Now."

The men rushed, not daring to waste a second. And within moments, they returned carrying baskets of ripe bananas, sweet mangoes, cooked grains, and clear water in bronze vessels.

Sitarama Raju approached the Sadhu again, this time his hand subtly dipping into the folds of his pocket.

From it, he pulled out a tiny cloth pouch-soft and heavy, the gentle clink of gold coins muffled within.

He stretched it forward, humble in posture.

"Sadhu... please. Accept this. For your guidance, for your presence."

The Sadhu opened one eye slightly, then smiled without mirth and shook his head.

"Oh Sitarama Raju... your helpful nature is admirable... but gold does not satisfy my hunger. Invite me to your home on every full moon and offer a complete meal-that will be enough."

Sitarama Raju lowered the pouch respectfully, understanding the depth of the Sadhu's words.

Then, folding his hands once more, he spoke with unwavering conviction.

"From this day on... as long as my bloodline lives... your grace shall receive food and fruit from our home. Daily. Without fail."

The Sadhu gave no reply, but his stillness itself was a blessing. A silence more meaningful than words. The wind, for the first time, seemed to calm... just a little.

As Sitaramaraju bent low to offer his final words of gratitude, a gentle rustle whispered through the air.

It was that haunting moment between sunset and darkness, when the sky holds its breath and shadows begin to sharpen. In that flicker of twilight, a torn, ancient parchment-small, yellowed, and folded a hundred times-drifted silently from beneath the Sadhu's crossed legs, landing at Sitaramaraju's feet.

He stared at it, the dimming light casting long shadows over the dry leaf as it settled-a whisper from fate.

He picked it up, cautiously.

The ink was old... nearly erased by time.

But as the last sunray slipped away, the name written on it flickered faintly, as if it had absorbed every drop of dusklight.

"MAHADHATRI"

[ADHRIKA]

The One who Sleeps Beneath the Roots.

A shiver passed through the gathered elders.

Sitaramaraju's voice cracked as he whispered, *"Mahadhatri"*

And without opening his eyes, the Sadhu finally spoke again:

"She is the last thread between this world... and the one your daughter may now walk."

The Search

Adhrika – The One Who Sleeps Beneath the Roots.

Before there was fear, there was silence.
Before there was silence, there was her.

She sleeps where no prayer dares to reach.

And now... she stirs.

Though her true name was Mahādhātri, the forest whispers her as Adhrika... the one unseen yet everywhere.

They stepped out of the temple as nightfall crept in. Shadows lengthened, and the air shifted.

The offerings of fruit and food laid before the Sadhu all week remained untouched-still sacred, still waiting.

Above them, the sky had melted into a gradient of fire and smoke. Orange bled into indigo, and darkness crawled in from the edges.

The air hung heavier now, as if it already knew what came next. Behind them, the temple stood like a silhouette from another time, forgotten by most, cursed by few.

They hadn't noticed it before.

The leaf.

Now, in the half-light of dusk, it rested in Sitarama Raju's hand-a message revealed only when the sun dipped low enough, its ink shimmering like blood dried under centuries.

He turned the leaf slowly, and on its back, etched into the veins by nature or curse, a riddle revealed itself:

"**<u>Mystery Riddle</u>** "

<u>"Near the Telugu Ganga's quiet shores,</u>
<u>Between Nandyal and Atmakur,</u>
<u>Something breathes beneath the trees.</u>
<u>Temples sleep inside the forest,</u>
<u>Too old to be remembered,</u>
<u>Too silent to be forgotten.</u>
<u>Some who visit find peace...</u>
<u>Others forget why they ever came."</u>

Sitarama Raju stared-eyes wide, mouth still, voice caught in his throat.

Eyes wide. Mouth still. Voice gone.

He wanted to ask the Sadhu, he should have asked the Sadhu.

But he didn't.

He'd only noticed the back of the leaf after stepping beyond the temple gates.

Now, his pride shackled his feet.

"How can I go back and ask him again?" he thought. *"It would make me look weak... desperate!"*

Still, he turned.

He went back.

And standing once more at the temple's threshold, he raised his voice into the gathering night-

"Sadhu!!"

"Sadhu, I need to ask you something-this riddle, what does it mean!?"

But the Sadhu didn't even glance up. He sat in still meditation, already drifted, it seemed, into another realm.

Sitarama Raju stepped back, defeated.

The pressure in his chest grew like fire caught behind his ribs.

That's when Abhimanyu stepped forward-not from the crowd, but from the shadows beyond, his presence not threatening, but perfectly timed.

From the dark shadows of the trees, walking slowly, with the dimming light casting long silhouettes behind him, came Abhimanyu.

He emerged from the side path, not hidden, not secretive-but always at a distance, as if watching all that unfolded near the Sadhu from a place untouched by attention.

He hadn't followed Sitarama Raju out of rebellion, nor did he fear stepping into the Sadhu's presence earlier.

He simply waited. Like a thread that knew when to tie itself. Now, as the air held its breath and even the leaves refused to rustle, he stepped into the fading light near the temple entrance.

He smiled faintly-half in jest, half in warmth-and said:
"Hello, Master Sitarama Raju ... do you need my help?"
His voice did hold sarcasm.

It held a certain intimate calm, like the moon whispering to the tide.

As he said that, he brought his two palms together and placed them near his lips,

gently blowing warm air between them-a simple act, but in the cold hush of twilight, it sounded like wind speaking to wood.

Sitarama Raju didn't speak immediately.

His breath was still caught in the strings of the riddle.

But Abhimanyu stepped closer, not too far, not too close.

"I saw you turn," he said. *"I knew you'd want to ask the Sadhu again."*

"But you didn't. So... maybe it's time you listen instead of ask."

He extended his hand forward-not to give, but to take.

The leaf shifted in the wind between their fingers, almost resisting. But Sitarama Raju let it go.

Abhimanyu, holding the leaf like an ancient truth, stared once...

Then twice...

Then raised his voice again.

He held the leaf close to his chest.

He didn't speak-

Not to the people.

Not to his brother.

Inside his mind, the riddle echoed louder than before.

The words echoed in his head-

Like the wind chanting through empty corridors.

He swallowed hard.

And then, he walked with his brother-Sitarama Raju, toward the line of servants.

Their steps are slow. The sky is almost done bleeding its orange.

They didn't speak. The silence between them said enough. The rest of the crowd, seeing the brothers move, began to gather again.

The Mansion was not far now. Just beyond the hillock.

A tea stall, lit by a flickering lantern, stood at the curve of the road.

The village heads and some servants, exhausted by tension, drifted toward it. The tea guy, a bent old man with glass-rimmed eyes, began pouring hot chai into glass tumblers with practiced elegance.

As he did, the brothers arrived.

The younger one, still holding the leaf, stepped into the middle of the group.

Steam from tea curled in the air.

Lantern light blinked against the growing night.

The leaf-its ink now darker than before, like it fed on dusk-stood in his grip.

He raised his voice.

Louder this time. Steadier.

From the chest. From every bone.

Like he wanted every ear-every shadow-to listen.

"Near the Telugu Ganga's quiet shores,
between Nandyal and Atmakur,
something breathes beneath the trees.
Temples sleep inside the forest,
Too old to be remembered,
Too silent to be forgotten.
Some who visit find peace...
Others forget why they ever came."

Dragging at Every Sentence End, Making Eye Contact Around him and Turning around Himself while he was Reading With the Riddle From the Leaf.

At first, nothing, then-a shudder. A ripple. Not in the ground, but through the people.

Every face twitched.

Every back slightly stiffened.

A tremble-small but collective.

And then, as if they all caught the same cold wind, everyone exhaled at once.

"Ayy, again with that damn riddle," someone muttered among Servants or village Heads."

"Just a line from some forgotten folk tale, isn't it?"

Their expressions said it all, Nervous mockery. Brushed-off fear. The kind that people use to hide real fear underneath.

But now... someone else stirred.

The tea shop owner, his back still to them, froze mid-pour.

The final drop of chai overfilled a tumbler and hissed onto the wood stove.

He didn't turn right away.

Instead, in a voice low, uneven, and edged with a memory not yet healed, he said:

"I've heard this before..."

And then he turned, eyes not quite meeting theirs, but looking somewhere... distant.

"I don't remember where. But that riddle... that line..."

"I heard it before a girl went missing, long ago. No one believed me then either."

A sudden, hollow quiet fell.

Even the lantern's flame flickered lower.

The tea shop owner stood still, chai still dripping from the overfilled cup on the stove.

He finally turned to face them fully, and with a dry voice-half whisper, half warning-he said:

"I... I don't know the answer to the riddle."

"But I know this much, it's this village. This riddle belongs there."

A few people blinked.

Then came the voice of one of the village heads, arms crossed, one eyebrow cocked higher than the other. His tone was thick with sarcasm:

"Oh, really? You think we didn't know that?"

"We live here, man. We've heard every weird tale, every nonsense rhyme. Don't talk like you found some secret."

The tea stall man didn't flinch. He just stared back, eyes slightly fogged, voice calmer now:

"That's what we all thought... back then, too."

The moment hung there—unmoving—like a spider's thread in still air.

Sitarama Raju looked around.

The Riddle.

The Sadhu.

The Ribbon girl.

His Daughter.

This wasn't about tales anymore.

Abhimanyu tightened his grip on the leaf again, the veins in the dried surface catching the lantern's glow. And Sitarama Raju-silently, without even noticing, took a step closer to him.

No more running in circles.

Abhimanyu looked at the tea shop owner and asked:

"What happened then?,

When you heard the riddle... before?"

The old man just stared back.

Then, quietly-like peeling back a secret he wasn't supposed to know-he spoke:

"The village... it lies to the East of our cemetery."

Everyone turned to look at him now, truly look. Even the sarcastic village head's smirk faltered.

The tea guy wiped his hands on the lower back of his shirt, as if suddenly uncomfortable with the weight of their attention.

"I'm not saying I know the riddle," he added, his eyes darting to the leaf still clutched in Abhimanyu's hand.

"But that name... that phrase... something in it matches what the elders used to whisper during storms."

He hesitated, then said it.

"It says... the Telugu Ganga Reservoir, somewhere between Nandyal and Atmakur... they called it **Vellugodu.** *That's all I know."*

Silence.

Not a leaf rustled.

Not a spoon clinked.

Even the chai steaming from the kettles felt like it froze for a second.

The village heads froze, expressions locked in a strange blend of disbelief and fear.

Sitarama Raju's jaw tightened.

Abhimnanyu stopped mid-breath, his lips still parted in mid-riddle.

The words had finally connected, a place... a real place.

One of the elder servants stammered, *"Vellugodu? That... that's..."*

One of the older men, his hands trembling as he held the rim of his steaming clay cup, leaned in closer and muttered under his breath,

"I heard of that village... not because of its water or trees... but because it's where witches live."

Everyone turned toward him.

He didn't blink, just stared down into his tea as if it might swallow him.

"Some say that land breeds the unnatural. That the very soil there holds whispers. Witches don't just hide there-they thrive there. Multiply. The forest bends for them."

Another man chimed in, more cautious, voice barely audible over the crackling coal stove:

"They say a witch once led them... maybe it was Adhrika. She isn't the only one-they whisper she's just the one who lets herself be seen."

The tea vendor's hands had stilled, the kettle left to whisper its steam into the silence, as he spoke in a low, gravelly voice.

"If she's truly part of this... she's there. That place isn't just a name in riddles. It's real. And she's waiting."

Sitarama Raju slowly looked up at the leaf again. That cursed, delicate thing that had caused this tremble in the air.

His brother stepped forward, his voice no longer a whisper but a steady, unshakable promise that cut through the murmurs:

"Then that's where we go. No matter what waits for us there."

The air around them felt heavier, but the flame of resolve had been lit.

ᗞᗞᗞ

The Abhimanyu's words hung in the air, and for a heartbeat, no one moved

The villagers glanced at one another, unease tightening their faces. Some shifted uncomfortably, others gripped their teacups a little harder.

The wind stirred again-subtle, but purposeful-carrying the scent of wet soil, old bark, and something deeper... something that had waited too long to be found.

Beneath the shivering rustle of banyan leaves, a hush fell.

Sitarama Raju, still silent, simply nodded once-slow, heavy and started walking forward, past the tea shop, past the murmuring crowd.

Each step he took seemed to pull the others with him, as though the very earth had decided this path alongside him.

One by one, the village heads, the servants, and Abhimanyu fell into step behind him.

No more talk.

No more doubts.

Only the fading light, the whisper of forgotten forests ahead... and the road to Vellugodu waiting to swallow them whole.

The road back to the mansion was quiet.

The sky had slipped fully into night now, painting the world in deep indigo and soft whispers of moonlight. Lanterns flickered along the muddy path, lighting the way as the group walked in a slow, thoughtful procession.

The tea shop had faded behind them. Now, only the crunch of gravel and the chirping of night insects followed them.

As they neared the gates of the Grand old Mansion, Sitarama Raju slowed down. The towering estate loomed under the moon's pale gaze - a silhouette of lost grandeur and restless hope.

He turned to face the group, the weary servants, the hesitant village heads, and his quiet but ever-watchful Abhimanyu.

With a deep breath, Sitarama Raju spoke.

"It's been wonderful... truly."

His voice was steady, though the grief still clung to its edges.

"That each of you stands with me in the search for my daughter... It's a reminder that even in darkness, light remains among us."

He paused, his eyes moving over every face.

"I have hope... that she will be found. And that whatever waits ahead — forest or flame, witch or riddle — we'll face it together."

There was no applause. No fanfare.

But there was respect.

A few nodded. A few lowered their heads. And some, quietly, looked toward the distant east... where the trees waited.

The night air wrapped around them like a thick velvet cloak.

The distant howl of a jackal faded into the endless silence of the fields.

Sitarama Raju stood tall at the mansion's gate, the heavy stone pillars rising like silent sentinels beside him.

The tired faces of the servants and village heads waited for his final words, the golden oil lamps flickering in their hands.

Slowly, almost solemnly, Sitarama Raju lifted his hand.

The movement was gentle, but in the cold hush of the night, it was like a command.

Every rustle stopped. Every whispered breath fell silent.

His palm faced outward, not as a ruler commanding, but as a father pleading.

His voice, when it came, was steady but laced with the ache of a wounded heart:

"It has been wonderful that everyone stands with me in the search for my daughter.

I hope... I believe... she will be found soon."

He took a breath, eyes glinting under the starlight.

"Come tomorrow morning... when the first shadows fade. We search in every forsaken corner, every breath of mist.

For now... go. Rest your bodies.

And thank you-truly-for standing with me."

He lowered his hand slowly.

The crowd bowed slightly, murmuring blessings under their breath.

The men faded into the night, their torchlights blinking one by one, swallowed by the misty road back to the village.

And Sitarama Raju and Abhimanyu stood a moment longer, alone, staring into the sleeping trees where tomorrow's fate awaited.

Inside the Mansion — *Midnight Weight*

Sitarama Raju stood alone at the grand entrance, watching the last footsteps of his people fade into the misty night. The great iron gates of the mansion groaned closed behind him, sealing him inside a world far colder than the night outside.

Without a word, he turned toward the vast stone corridor.

The weight of regret — heavier than his own body — made him lean against the ancient walls, dragging one hand along the dusty pillars for support. His steps were slow, echoing faintly through the empty halls.

He was not sick. His body was strong as ever.

But it was his heart...

The ache of imagining a morning without his daughter's smile...

A day without her little footsteps pattering across the marble floors...

That crushed the air from his lungs with every breath he took.

The flickering oil lamps cast long, broken shadows on the walls, distorting his figure, making him look like a fallen titan from a forgotten age.

Each hallway he crossed, each stair he climbed, memories clung to him like heavy chains:

—Her laughter bouncing off these same walls,

—Her tiny fingers tugging at his robes,

—The way she would hide behind the grand pillars during games.

By the time he reached the door to his suite, his body had almost given up and was about to faint on the stairs. Abhimanyu came from behind, grabbed him in his bare hands, and said, *"I got you, brother,"* before carrying him into the suite. As they entered, he added, *"I'll always be there for you, even at your worst-to combat the battle with you."*

With a heavy push of his shoulder, Abhimanyu forced the door open.

The grand suite creaked in surrender, its silence deeper than sleep. The ornate bed, regal tapestries, and glistening chandeliers shimmered under the dim lights, but none of it held meaning anymore. The luxury felt lifeless-just empty echoes of what once was.

Abhimanyu walked in slowly, his eyes hollow, his steps heavy. Without a word, he changed his brother into nightwear with gentle care, as though tucking away a memory. He lifted the blanket and draped it over him, smoothing it out at the corners.

Then, he turned toward the tall glass doors.

With a soft pull, the balcony windows opened.
Cool night air swept into the room, brushing the curtains like ghostly hands.
Abhimanyu stepped forward and stood still.
From the edge of the marble balcony, he gazed up, eyes fixed on the stars, a sky too distant to offer comfort.

He didn't speak. He didn't cry.
Just stood-still and silent-as though trying to hear something buried in the stars.

Then, quietly, he turned back. Walked in. Closed the balcony doors behind him.

And as he left the room...
The winds softened... the night deepened.

4

The Sinister I

---❦---

<u>Morning crept in slowly, draping the sky in a pale gold.</u>

The birds chimed sweetly across the trees, just like any other day-yet something was different.

The domestic animals inside the mansion-the cows, buffaloes, goats, and hens-were eerily still.

Their usual liveliness was missing.

Their heads drooped, their movements sluggish, almost grieving.

The mansion, which once woke to the innocent chaos of her tiny footsteps, now felt like a hollow temple.

Sitarama Raju had awoken even before the hens' first crow.

Long before the horizon could even think of brightening, he was already stirring - his heavy heart beating a march louder than any morning drum.

This time,

No waiting for servants,

no drawn-out preparation.

He moved swiftly, almost fiercely, through the grand halls of the mansion —

Wrapping his shawl tightly around his shoulders as he

reached the stone-walled bathing space.

With no hesitation, he unwrapped, set the brass bucket beneath the hanging copper pot, and tugged the chain.

A burst of cold water cascaded down, hitting his bare skin like needles —

shocking him awake, but never quite numbing the ache in his chest.

He stood still under it, jaw clenched, water trickling down his face like silent tears.

Each drop seemed to carry the weight of grief and fury, soaking his hair, his shoulders, his spine.

The silence was deafening - only the dripping echo and his own breath filled the chamber.

Then, without pause, he stepped out.

The cold still clinging to him, he reached for the coarse towel, wiped his face,

tightened the knot of his cloth belt with firm, practiced hands —

and slid his trusted dagger into his waistband.

It's cold, hilt pressed against his skin,

as if reminding him - today, he would not be the man who waits.

The trail to Vellugodu, the so-called Witch Village, awaited.

And today, he would lead.

No matter what the riddles said.

No matter what, cursed whispers wrapped the village's name.

Sitarama Raju would march into the forested unknown.

For her.

For his daughter.

One by one, the village heads, servants, and Abhimanyu arrived - wrapped in shawls, carrying sticks, lanterns, and supplies for the trail ahead.

Their faces were grim but determined.

As they gathered near the mansion gate with their supplies, Sitarama Raju watched from the balcony above, his figure almost ghost-like in the morning haze.

He was dressed but regally, a cloth belt tied around his waist to keep the early chill away.

His eyes, deep with worry and fire, narrowed as he saw the trail party preparing below.

With quiet frustration burning inside him, he reached into the folds of his belt and pulled out the small diamond-shaped box - the same one from before.

Opening it with a flick of his thumb, he took out a cigar, placed it between his lips, and lit it with a single scratch of a match.

He dragged it hard, the smoke curling against the mansion's ancient walls.

For a moment, he leaned against the cool stone, lost in the bitterness of the tobacco and the heavier bitterness in his chest.

Halfway through the cigar, his hand trembled slightly.

A memory flashed - his daughter's small hands slapping the cigar from his fingers once, laughing and scolding him with innocent anger.

She hated the smoke.

She hated the smell.

A sudden guilt tore through him.

He yanked the cigar from his lips, threw it down onto the balcony floor, and smashed it under his own bare foot, grinding it into the stone with a grimace - both from pain and shame.

Without a word, he turned on his heel, walking into the mansion and up to his room.

There, the man who once led armies prepared for a different kind of battle.

He dressed in a pure white linen shirt, slightly see-through in the morning light, with a simple inner banyan worn underneath-paired with a clean white dhoti (panche) tucked sharply at the waist, and soft brown sandals to match. His look was traditional and dignified, like the proud elders of the land who commanded respect with mere presence.

After getting dressed, he stood before the dusty mirror, adjusted the tiger claw necklace hanging against his chest, and stared into his own eyes-deep, tired, but burning with an unbroken flame.

In the stillness of the room, he whispered firmly:

"Sitarama Raju... You can do it. No matter what trouble comes your way... we will break it down and find our little Daughter."

With a final tug at his waistband, he grabbed the heavy wall gun from its rack and stormed down to the living room, where the gathering crowd awaited him.

Without wasting a moment, his voice rang out-sharp and commanding:

"We leave at once. Follow the eastward path. The quicker we move, the quicker we find her."

The air grew tense.

Outside, the blue and gold carts stood ready, the horses snorting clouds of mist into the crisp morning.

Standing apart from the others was Sitarama Raju's special steed —

A magnificent black horse, towering with powerful muscles gleaming under the soft morning sun.

It was a rare breed he had once brought back from his travels to Italy, a gift from a European count — a stallion known for its wild spirit and endless stamina.

Its silky mane fluttered in the cold breeze, and its fierce black eyes glistened with a warrior's soul.

Sitarama Raju paused for a moment.

For the first time in many days, a tiny flicker of pride lifted his heavy heart.

He settled his mustache with a slow, proud stroke, gazing at the horse with a small, almost unnoticeable smile —

as if saying in his heart,

"It's my horse. My companion."

Without hesitation, he swung up onto the saddle with the agility of a man much younger.

The horse stamped its hooves powerfully, eager for the trail ahead.

From his high seat, Sitarama Raju looked down at everyone gathered —

The village heads gripping their sticks and staffs,

The servants are tightening the ropes on the supply carts,

The young men are adjusting their cloth belts.

Everyone was ready.

The trail would be long, but the spirit was unbroken.

Just as Sitarama Raju was about to signal the start of their march,

Abhimanyu stepped forward quickly and stopped him, raising a hand.

Sitarama Raju tightened his grip on the reins, the black stallion shifting under him impatiently.

He frowned slightly as Abhimanyu, a lean, sharp-eyed man-stepped closer, one hand raised respectfully but urgently.

"Brother..." he said, voice low but firm,

As Sitarama Raju settled on his mighty black horse, surveying the line of carts and men,

Abhimanyu grinned mischievously and called out,

"Where is my seat, brother?"

Without turning much, Sitarama Raju replied coolly,

"You can sit in the cart back there."

He pointed casually to a cart laden with supplies.

But when do younger brothers ever listen to elder ones?

The younger brother smirked, shook his head playfully, and made a cheeky gesture, pointing at Sitarama Raju's horse —

Indicating he would come riding with him, behind his back.

Sitarama Raju giggled like an overgrown child and even threw a teasing smile at one of the nearby servants.

The servant, understanding the silent message immediately, chuckled back and rushed toward the mansion.

Moments later, the servant returned with another leather seat, an attachable saddle and quickly fastened it behind Sitarama Raju's main saddle with skilled hands.

Within a minute, it was ready.

Sitarama Raju, still sitting tall and stern on his horse, extended his strong hand downward and said with a rare softness in his voice,

"Come, join Brother.

We will return with our little Daughter."

Abhimanyu reached up, and as their hands met, they clapped together with such force that it echoed sharply across the mansion yard —

A sound full of brotherhood, strength, and a deep, silent promise.

With a firm pull, Sitarama Raju hauled him up onto the back seat, both of them now sitting together astride the magnificent black horse.

Meanwhile, around them:

The servants tightened the ropes on the supply carts.

The village's young men adjusted their cloth belts, checked their sticks, and ensured their lanterns were secured.

Everyone was ready.

The mist still clung to the earth.

The horses pawed the ground restlessly.

Sitarama Raju leaned forward, tightened his grip on the reins, and with a nod to his brother, said in a voice that rumbled like the earth before a storm:

"Let's bring her home."

And with that, the first hoofbeats struck the wet earth as the trail to the Old Temple began.

Sitarama Raju's horse was the first to exit the mansion gates, riding tall and determined on his black stallion. Behind him, the village heads, the servants, and the heavy supply carts followed - a slow, solemn procession against the morning mist.

But just as they crossed the old stone arch near the estate wall, something unexpected happened —

Abhimanyu, with a mischievous glint in his eye, pressed his left leg twice gently against the horse's side.

The stallion, trained to respond to such signals, instantly veered left, off the main trail.

Startled, Sitarama Raju turned his head sharply and growled,

"Why did you give the wrong direction to the horse?
We were supposed to go right!"

Abhimanyu chuckled, his voice light and playful,

"No, Brother.
I thought... maybe first, we should meet the Sadhu and take his blessings before stepping into the unknown."

Sitarama Raju stared at him for a long second, frustration fighting with reluctant admiration —

And then, without a word, he yanked the reins, guiding the horse properly along the hidden forest path that led toward the old temple.

As they approached, the temple revealed itself from the morning shadows —

Ancient, moss-covered, with broken stone statues guarding its crumbling stairway.

There, deep in the heart of the temple courtyard, sat the Sadhu —

Silent as a mountain, unmoving beneath a natural arch formed by two intertwined banyan trees.

His body draped in ochre cloth, his hair wild and matted, his figure blending into the roots and branches as though he were part of the very earth.

All around him, the offerings of fruits and food left by villagers, half-eaten now by monkeys, birds, or perhaps forest raccoons.

The brothers exchanged a glance but said nothing.

Such things were not considered disrespectful; nature was nature.

Without dismounting at first, Sitarama Raju called out, his voice low but firm,

"Sadhu Maharaj... We are leaving.
We only came seeking your blessings."

The Sadhu did not stir from his meditation —

His body as still as stone, his mind lost in the mists of some higher realm.

Respectfully, both brothers dismounted quietly.

They moved toward the great banyan trees that framed the Sadhu —

Each brother stepped away from the other, walking in opposite directions.

Toward the twin banyan trees, ancient and colossal, their roots entwined like serpents, rising above the earth to form a majestic archway.

The branches curled and stretched like arms of forgotten gods, casting long shadows on the forest floor. Moss clung to their trunks, and vines draped like threads of time.

At the top of the arch, where the trees met like clasped hands in prayer, the Sadhu sat in silent meditation —

His figure cloaked in stillness, a wooden staff resting beside him, his hair flowing like rivers of ash, eyes closed as if hearing the forest breathe.

As they approached, the brothers stretched out their arms.

Each one placed their hands gently on the low branches of the banyan before them —

a sacred gesture of taking blessings from these living giants. The trees, silent yet sentient, bore witness to the reverence of those who now stepped beneath them.

Beyond the arch, the forest dimmed.

The overgrowth gave way to a forgotten path that led to the ancient temple — stone pillars swallowed in moss, its entry dark, foreboding, yet quietly waiting.

The Sadhu did not move.

But something in the air stirred-a hush, as if the very forest had paused.

Instead of disturbing the holy man, they chose to bow before the roots and low-hanging branches, drawing the blessing from the sacred nature itself.

The air around them buzzed softly - a timeless energy —

As if the very trees acknowledged their prayer.

After a brief moment of silence, Sitarama Raju turned toward the servants who had caught up behind them and ordered,

"Leave a box of fruits and food here.

For him or the animals let them have it. It will serve its purpose."

The servants obeyed immediately, placing the box carefully at the edge of the temple steps.

Without another word, the brothers remounted their horse,

Their white linen clothes brushing softly against the horse's sleek black hide, their hearts steadier now, bolstered by unseen blessings.

Slowly, the group turned away from the temple and began riding toward their next destination —

The village cemetery.

ᕫᕫᕫ

The village cemetery.

Where whispers of old souls awaited them...

And the fog grew thicker with each step.

The journey from the temple back to the village paths was slow and heavy.

The black stallion's hooves thudded deep into the dry, cracking earth, sending faint echoes across the fields.

As Sitarama Raju and Abhimanyu rode tall and proud through the dusty village streets, heads began to pop out from doorways - old women with their hair tied back, men in lungis resting on charpoys, little children barefoot and wide-eyed.

Some of these people hadn't even been born when Sitarama Raju had first built his estate.

They had only heard stories-whispered rumours-about the "House of Sitarama Raju" and how its men rode out only for matters of life and death.

A low murmur passed through the crowds like a ripple through water:

"They're going to see the Witch..."

"His Daughter has gone missing... now the old spirits will awaken..."

The villagers backed away respectfully, yet with an unmistakable fear in their eyes.

Mothers pulled their children inside; old priests muttered hasty prayers under their breath.

The thudding of the stallion's hooves grew louder, heavier —

THUMP... THUMP.. THUMP

Almost like a war drum announcing something grim.

Dust rose in their wake, cloaking the air in a soft, brown fog,

until only the silhouette of Sitarama Raju and his brother remained - two figures against the rising sun.

The road narrowed as they approached the edge of the village —

A place few dared to visit after dark: the village cemetery.

The old cemetery loomed ahead, half-swallowed by creeping vines and skeletal trees.

The crooked gravestones jutted out like broken teeth from the earth, and a crooked iron gate, rusted and screeching with every wind, marked the entrance.

Black crows circled above, their calls sharp and unpleasant.

A strange coldness wrapped around the group, a sudden shift from the warm morning air to something... older.

Something that did not belong to the living.

Sitarama Raju tightened his jaw and held the reins firmly.

Beside him, Abhimanyu, usually playful - grew silent, his face hardening with a seriousness not usual for his age.

The carts rumbled behind them, wheels creaking, while the servants and villagers dared not make a sound.

As they passed through the creaking cemetery gate, the earth seemed to sigh under the weight of their arrival.

They had come seeking answers...

But the land of the dead had its own secrets to keep.

The heavy carts halted just outside the cemetery's broken iron gate. The horses snorted nervously, their hooves stamping the earth as if sensing something wrong. The servants exchanged wary glances, but none dared speak.

Sitarama Raju remained mounted, his eyes scanning the overgrown graveyard with a soldier's precision.

But Abhimanyu, without hesitation, swung one leg over and hopped down from the horse, his boots crunching against the brittle grass and loose stones beneath him.

With a quick motion, he reached into his side satchel and pulled out a small, aged compass —

Italian-made, gifted by a wandering merchant years ago.

The brass casing was scratched and dulled with time,

and the dial inside had a strange beauty:

Half of the North pointer was painted a deep, rusted red, the other half a polished silver.

Abhimanyu flipped the lid open with a click.

The needle trembled slightly, then settled with a slow, reluctant spin -

pointing east, just beyond the oldest part of the cemetery.

Sitarama Raju narrowed his eyes from atop the horse.

"You're using that old thing?" he asked, voice low but amused.

Abhimanyu smirked without looking up, dusting dirt from his sleeves.

"It's old, yes," he replied, *"but it still knows which way the living shouldn't go... and where we must."*

He knelt briefly, pressing the compass flat against a cracked tombstone to steady it.

The direction was clear: east-toward a dense patch of trees and crumbling graves that seemed untouched for decades.

The air around them felt heavier now, almost thick enough to choke.

The servants shifted uneasily behind them, and even the horses jerked their heads as if protesting the path ahead.

But Abhimanyu rose calmly, snapping the compass closed with a soft metallic click.

He dusted his palms together and looked back up at Sitarama Raju, giving a short nod:

"This way, brother.

The real trail... starts beyond the dead."

Without wasting another moment, Abhimanyu led the way, stepping carefully among the leaning stones,

His compass was gripped tightly in his hand.

But just as they crossed deeper into the cemetery's heart,

Sitarama Raju, steady and towering only moments ago, suddenly swayed on his horse.

His breath hitched,

his eyes blinked rapidly,

and a wave of dizziness crushed through his mind like a heavy tide.

He leaned forward helplessly, his body slumping against the horse's mane.

Before anyone could process it,

he slid halfway off the horse, unconscious,

his hand slipping from the reins.

"Brother!!"

Abhimanyu shouted, panic flashing across his face.

Without a second thought, he rushed forward, his boots barely touching the ground —

Reaching Sitarama Raju just in time, grabbing his collapsing body with both arms.

The world seemed to freeze.

The procession behind them gasped,

the carts rattled to an awkward stop,

and a cold shiver ran through the servants and village Heads.

They had never seen Sitarama Raju, the pillar of their world-fall like this.

In seconds, everyone surrounded him, murmuring in alarm.

"Bring water!" barked one of the elder servants, urgency cutting through the air.

A younger servant, hands trembling, raced to fetch a jug.

He poured a little water into the cupped palms of Abhimanyu, who carefully sprinkled a few drops onto Sitarama Raju's forehead and lips.

With a desperate gasp for air, he woke up again

Sitarama Raju's chest lifted, and his eyes snapped open wide, as if waking from a drowning nightmare.

Everyone exhaled in relief.

Still dazed but alive, Sitarama Raju blinked rapidly, focusing on his brother's worried face above him.

Abhimanyu gave him a grim but reassuring smile,

squeezing his arm firmly.

"You're alright, brother. Just breathe. You're with us.

And we have a little one to bring back... Home," he whispered.

The old warrior struggled upright with help,

But before the servants could lift him fully, while still in his brother's steady arms,

Sitarama Raju's voice cracked like an old branch under pressure as he gasped out,

His eyes were wide, staring into something no one else could see:

"I saw her face... she wasn't a stranger...

She was someone... someone from long before....(Gasping)

Before I was even born,

*It was **Tantri**,*

I'd know her even among a million souls,

It was Tantri who took our Little Girl...."

As the name escaped his lips, thick clouds rolled across the sky, blotting out the pale morning sun.

A deep shadow draped itself over the cemetery, turning the world colder, dimmer, as if nature itself recoiled.

The wind stirred without warning, rising in sudden, sharp gusts that tugged violently at the men's shawls and the horses' manes.

Sitarama Raju's white linen shirt flared to one side, the cloth belts and turbans of the villagers fluttering toward the east, the direction of their march.

Even the ancient trees lining the cemetery seemed to groan and lean, bowing under the invisible weight of the moment, as if the earth had just heard the forbidden name whispered again after decades of silence.

He clutched tighter to his brother's arm,

his next words almost a broken whisper, as if reliving a moment torn from the deepest nightmare:

"Before they vanished... I saw it-her smile.

Not the smile of a person... but the smile of something dark... something that was waiting for this moment... for years."

The weight of the revelation crashed down on the group.

Even the servants who had seen battle and famine turned pale.

Without hesitation, his younger brother and the nearest servants lifted Sitarama Raju properly to his feet,

steadying him with fierce care.

One servant murmured a prayer under his breath.

Another looked instinctively over his shoulder,

as if half-expecting the shadows themselves to crawl toward them.

Sitarama Raju, swaying but refusing to fall again,

nodded once, hard and slow.

The carts creaked forward.

The horses stamped the earth nervously.

There was no turning back now.

Not after what he had seen.

Not after knowing who...or what... waited for them ahead.

The trail into the thick woods loomed in front of them,

and Vellugodu's haunted borders beckoned like a whisper in the mist...

Before they could move further, Abhimanyu quickly stepped forward, concern heavy in his voice.

"Brother, come sit in the cart with the village Heads. You need your strength. Let us carry you to the battle that awaits."

The village heads, firm and respectful, nodded in agreement, urging Sitarama Raju with softened eyes.

For a brief second, the old warrior hesitated-pride battling necessity, but then, with a quiet sigh and a sharp nod, he agreed.

Supported by his brother and two servants, Sitarama Raju climbed into the cart, settling among the supplies, wrapping his fingers around the edge of the wooden frame like a general still at the head of his army.

Meanwhile, his brother, his spirit ablaze, swung himself up onto Sitarama Raju's great black horse, the beast snorting and stamping the ground as if sensing the rising fire in its new rider.

Gripping the reins tight, Abhimanyu raised his voice, roaring across the field with a thunder that struck every heart:

"For Our Daughter!"

Abhimanyu pulled the reins sharply to his chest. The black horse immediately rose onto its two strong back legs, lifting its front hooves high into the air. The morning mist wrapped around them, and for a moment, the horse and rider looked like a single towering figure against the fog. The horse let out a loud snort, its muscles tense, ready to charge forward. The village watched as the Abhimanyu steadied the horse, set his jaw, and pushed them all into motion toward the forest trail.

The villagers tightened their grips on their sticks and staffs, the servants pulled their carts into formation, and the caravan surged forward, diving into the jaws of the misty forest where shadows whispered secrets and the unknown awaited.

ᗡᗡᗡ

As the rally moved deeper into the woods, the rhythm of marching carts, horses, and boots echoed through the thickening trees. It had been over three hours since they'd left the mansion-no breaks, no stops.

The villagers shared fruits and raw vegetables passed between carts, trying to keep their strength.

But Sitarama Raju didn't touch anything. He leaned back against a thick pillow in the blue-and-gold cart, his eyes open, heavy with stress, never fully resting. His mind looped the same thought again and again:
What do I do next? Where do I go?

But Abhimanyu didn't eat. He didn't speak. He didn't even pause his ride.

From the very beginning of the journey, he had ridden ahead
horse galloping strong, dust trailing behind him-
never slowing, never resting.
The reins gripped tight in his calloused hands, eyes sharp and forward, as if he were chasing time itself.

His endurance was nothing short of madness.
To ride so long, without food, without a single drop of water
—
yet still look carved from stone, it was inhuman.

Even the others began whispering.

Something about Abhimanyu's strength that day felt as if it wasn't just his own.

Still, it was just 90 kilometres of travel. As they pushed ahead, a worn wooden board came into view , painted in bold, fading white letters:

"Vellugodu Reservoir – 200m Ahead"

The march slowed slightly. They could now see the broad stone steps climbing up to the reservoir's edge as they passed through the narrow path. One of the village heads pointed forward and called out, "Let's stop near any shop if we find one. We can get some information."

Just beside the dam, a small roadside shop gave off a sharp scent of fish and smoke. Freshly caught fish from the reservoir's outlet hung on hooks, while a large frying pan sizzled on an iron stove.

The group slowed. Hooves paused. Wheels came to a halt.

One of the servants, seated at the front riding bench of a cart, jumped down and approached the shop. He casually nodded to the vendor and said, "One fried fish.", he said with Simple and Sweet.

The shopkeeper, a rugged man in his late forties with fish scales on his fingers, nodded and began preparing the fish-slicing, salting, and tossing it into the bubbling oil. As it hissed and sizzled, the servant leaned closer and asked quietly,

"Do you know... any old witch who lives around here?"

The shopkeeper didn't look up. He just kept slicing.

"There are many Witches & B!tches here," he replied after a beat, *"Name One and I will propose You One ?"*

The servant adjusted his shawl, pretending to look over the other fried fish, and without lifting his eyes, asked, *"What about... Adhrika?"*

At that moment, that very name, everything stopped for the shopkeeper.

His face froze. He gripped the spoon too tightly. In a split second, his hand slipped, and the ladle dropped into the oil. A sharp splash sent hot oil spilling over the side - a few drops landing straight on his exposed wrist.

He let out a stifled gasp, flinching, but not saying a word.

And that's when the servant knew the name meant something.

The shopkeeper, eyes now fixed and distant, slowly reached for a cloth and dabbed at the burn on his wrist, but his focus wasn't on the pain. His lips parted slightly, and for a moment, he didn't speak, as if debating whether to say what was on his mind.

Then, with a voice quieter than before, he leaned in toward the servant and muttered:

"Don't say that name so easily here... not near the water."

The man glanced around nervously, his eyes darting between trees and faces, making sure no one else was too close.

He leaned in slightly, lowering his voice to a near whisper.

"Adhrika... that woman hasn't aged in decades."

He paused, eyes scanning the surroundings once more, as if even the trees might be listening.
Only when he was sure no one could hear did he continue:

"She lives near the northern forest edge... in a broken structure, once a British rest house. No one dares go near it."

He turned his back, pretending to be busy himself with the fish again, then added, *"Some say she talks to animals. Others say she talks to the ones below the ground."*

Another hiss of oil filled the silence.

Then he handed over the fried fish, not meeting the servant's eyes this time.

"Take this. And if you know what's good for you... Don't go there at night."

The servant nodded silently to the shopkeeper and walked away without asking any more questions. The smell of fried fish clung to the paper in his hands, but the hunger that had once stirred in his belly was gone. His thoughts were heavier now.

He returned to the cart, where Sitarama Raju still leaned back on the cushions, eyes half-closed but alert. The servant held out the fish and said, calmly but firmly,

"Master, I didn't find the pieces of the puzzle... but I found the puzzle itself."

Sitarama Raju straightened immediately, reaching out to take the warm parcel. His eyes narrowed with interest, and he leaned forward, motioning for the servant to speak.

"Well, what does your puzzle say then?" he asked.

The servant looked around once, then spoke softly:

"My puzzle says this — Adhrika. That woman hasn't aged in decades. She lives near the northern forest edge. A broken structure... it was once a British rest house. No one dares go near it."

Sitarama Raju's grip on the wrapped fish tightened, and without even unwrapping it, he set it aside.

With a fire returning to his eyes, he barked out,

"Prepare everyone. We're moving now!"

by adjusting his Cousin at his lower back.

As the carts were readied again, one of the village heads stepped down and quietly approached the cart. He had been making quiet inquiries while the others were resting. Leaning in, he said, "Master Sitarama Raju ... I spoke to a few men I know around here. The location matches. She stays in that same British house, it's close to a farmland, the kind where they grow things they shouldn't. Ganja, tobacco... that sort. Just where the reservoir's outlet ends and flows toward the other side of the valley."

Sitarama Raju turned to his brother.

Abhimanyu had been there all along-silent, listening.

He didn't need to be told anything.

He had heard every word.
And he had already understood.

He met Sitarama Raju's gaze, not with shock, not with fear, but with a quiet fire burning behind his eyes.

There was no need for words.
The silence between them said enough.

They had a direction.

They had a name.

And now... they had very little time.

As they moved forward, the air began to shift.

5

The Sinister II

<u>The Scent Before the Shadows — Arrival at the British Mansion</u>

It was the sharp, unmistakable scent that hit them first, not of the forest, nor the dam, but of dried leaves and a bitter aroma. One of the servants leaned closer to the bush-lined path and whispered, "Weed plants... and tobacco too." Another confirmed with a slight nod, brushing his fingers over the leaf edge. The villagers exchanged uneasy glances, but Sitarama Raju, resting against the pillow inside the cart, let out a quiet chuckle. Though they couldn't see him, the way his laughter echoed inside the cart made them all smile knowingly. Even in such darkness, the old warrior hadn't lost his dry humor.

The narrow path gave way to a larger clearing, and there it stood — The British Rest House.

Abandoned for years, its whitewashed walls had faded into a patchy grey. Vines gripped the corners of the building, snaking across cracked stone and shattered windows. The gates in front were rusted, heavy, and half-consumed by weeds. Sitarama Raju, his brother, and a loyal servant approached first. With a combined push, the iron gates groaned —

A long, metallic creak that screamed through the silence, before slowly opening wide.

One by one, the rest followed behind, stepping cautiously into the compound.

It was silent inside. No dogs. No birds. Not even a rat in sight. The only movement came from the lazy swirling of houseflies dancing over old water stains on the porch walls. A sense of waiting, something unseen, hung in the stillness.

Then they saw him.

To the right side of the courtyard stood an old well, perfectly circular and carved in black stone. At its centre, attached to a rusted pulley hook, a four-layered hardened rope creaked with weight. An old man was drawing water, his grip firm, arms straining as he pulled. His back was hunched, his skin tanned and worn, but the strength in his movement spoke of a man used to labor, not yet broken by time.

He didn't look at them. Not at first.

Just kept drawing water, each pull echoing with effort, as the bucket climbed from the darkness below, glistening with cold, clear water drawn from the reservoir's outlet deep beneath the ground.

Sitarama Raju stepped forward, watching the man in silence, the breeze catching the ends of his shawl.

The old man stood steady beside the well, the rope taut in his strong, veined hands. When he saw Sitarama Raju approach, he lowered the bucket slowly and said,

"What do you want, my King?"

Sitarama Raju paused in his tracks, his brow tightening.

"Wait... did you just call me 'my King'? What makes you think I'm a king? The way I dress? Or is there something else?"

The old man gave a gentle, eerie smile.

"Our Lord sensed your scent the moment you entered this land. Your steps carried the weight of command. And tell me, what common man marches straight through <u>Vellugodu</u> and arrives here, without being swallowed by its whispers?"

Before anyone could question him further, a voice rang out sharply from above.

"Shut the funk up, old man!"

A girl leaned out of a dusty window, flicking her hair behind her ear with annoyance. Her skin had a calm, fair tone, her black curls brushed across her cheekbones, and her eyes narrowed with irritation. She wore a flowing black dress—not old-fashioned, but not modern either. Just... off.

"You keep blabbing the same creepy lines to anyone who comes here!"

She scanned the group. Her eyes sharpened.

"Come upstairs," she said flatly, then disappeared inside.

The heavy main doors creaked open. Two servants stayed to guard outside. The rest followed her up the grand staircase, lined with chipped bannisters, aged with dampness and vines. The wooden steps groaned under each footfall, every creak echoing through the once-glorious halls of the British mansion. Inside, faded portraits hung on cracked walls. The chandelier above hung crooked, its crystals dusty and dulled by time. A rusting grand piano sat untouched in the corner.

They entered a lounge, aged but regal. Torn velvet sofas, bookshelves with half-burnt candles, and one huge arched window facing the forest beyond.

A servant passed them water. She leaned against the pillar, arms folded, and got straight to it.

"So, what does your village want?"

Sitarama Raju sat up straight, eyes blazing. One word burst from his chest.

"Girl."

She was surprised by the word, yet a smirk played on her face-elegant, dangerous-as, as if she'd just uncovered a hidden piece of a puzzle only she could solve.

"What? We don't sell kids here, okay?! You old creep, I thought you had class by the way you walked in with that royal face, but now-wait(She paused), you want Girl, it's me in this Mansion"

She stepped forward, raising her hand with Aggression.

"You meant me? How dare you..."

But before her slap could land, her wrist froze mid-air. Her own arm betrayed her, locking in place. Her breath caught in her throat.

From behind, a gust of cold wind swept through the hall. Curtains fluttered wildly. A shimmer of gold dust circled the air... and she stepped in. But before her slap could land, her wrist froze mid-air. Her own arm betrayed her, locking in place. Her breath caught in her throat.

From behind, a gust of cold wind swept through the hall. Curtains fluttered wildly. A shimmer of gold dust circled the air... and she stepped in.

ADHRIKA

She wasn't ancient, but there was something timeless about her. Her dark blue sari flowed like smoke, edged with burnt orange and emerald beads. Her posture was graceful, but firm, like a teacher who had seen too much and said too little. Her eyes were a deep, unsettling green—like the forest itself—and her hands moved with slow precision.

Without touching the girl, she made a half-spiral motion with her fingers. The raised palm lowered itself.

*"That's enough, **TARA**".*

Her voice was calm, deep, and heavy with quiet power.

The room fell still.

Adhrika turned to Sitarama Raju.

"You came for the girl. You'll get your answers. But you must be prepared to hear the truth... even if it's not the one you want."

Adhrika turned sharply, her presence commanding the dimly lit room. Her voice, calm but direct, echoed off the old wooden walls of the British mansion as she stared at him, pointing firmly with her index finger.

"Abhimanyu, come inside. We need to talk."

The room fell still.

The aged wood of the old mansion groaned faintly, as if holding its breath.

Sitarama Raju halted mid-step. Abhimanyu's expression shifted. The village heads and elder servants stood frozen at the threshold.

All eyes turned to the young woman before them. The flicker of the lamp caught the edge of her earrings, her posture calm yet commanding.

Without acknowledging the tension, Adhrika casually pointed at Sitaramaju and asked:

"And you? What's your name, man?"

Silence fell like a curtain.

Even the village heads, long used to strange omens and ancient tales, stared wide-eyed. The servants shifted nervously. No one expected this. No one knew what to say.

Before they could react, Adhrika smirked, brushing her hair behind her ear with a dismissive wave.

"Oh come on... how would I know you?" she shrugged, then turned to Abhimanyu, her tone sharpening:

*"But you-you studied in London, didn't you? Four years, right? Near Kensington. You used to hang around that **café**... **Matflin**, I think?"*

Abhimanyu, still trying to process everything, blinked fast... and then it hit him.

"Wait... Matflin Café? That fire accident?"

She nodded slowly.

"Yes. You saved me once. You don't remember, do you?"

Abhimanyu laughed awkwardly and scratched the back of his neck.

"I do remember saving someone Old ... but you look younger than I remember. I mean, the woman I carried out-she was kinda heavy & Old."

The room chuckled nervously, breaking some of the tension, but Adhrika didn't laugh.

Instead, she stepped forward, eyes sharper now, as though peeling back layers of memories they didn't know they had.

Adhrika turned around without waiting for a reply and began walking up the creaky wooden staircase, her steps deliberate, echoing faintly under the high ceiling. The worn bannister was still lined with faded gold carvings, and cobwebs danced gently in the corners with each gust of wind slipping through the broken window panes. A large, arched window filtered pale light across the stairway, casting long shadows across the cracked tiles.

She opened the door at the top with a light push; it groaned but obeyed. Inside was a spacious room dimly lit by an oil lamp on a heavy desk. The ceiling fan above turned slowly, its blades cutting through the still air with a lazy rhythm. Old furniture lined the room: a grandfather clock, an antique shelf with books coated in dust, and a tall mirror draped with an embroidered cloth.

"Come in," she said, voice softer now. *"Let's talk in here. We'll be left alone."*

Sitarama Raju stepped in first, his eyes scanning every corner of the room like a war general walking into an ambush. Abhimanyu followed, more casual but still trying to piece together the bizarre feeling that she already knew them. Behind them, the village heads and elder servants entered in silence, their eyes wide with caution and curiosity.

Each step they took into the mansion felt like stepping into a place pulled from a dream... or a warning.

She sat down on a cushioned chair and gestured for Sitarama Raju and Abhimanyu to take the two wooden seats in front of her.

The others stood quietly behind them, forming a loose semicircle, their presence steady but respectful.

A servant placed a steel tray with water glasses on a side table, then exited the room, shutting the door behind him with a low thud.

Adhrika leaned forward.

"Now. You said you want a girl. Is She Lost, or do you want the girl to be in your Control? That's why you're here, right?"

Sitaramaju nodded slowly, locking eyes with her.

"Yes. She was taken. And we were told... someone in this house may know something."

She tilted her head slightly, watching him like a puzzle she wasn't sure she wanted to solve just yet.

Sitaramaju and Abhimanyu exchanged a sharp glance-startled, cautious.

Abhimanyu asked, *"How do you know all this? Who told you?"*

Adhrika smirked, leaned back in her chair, and without blinking said—

"Because I'm a witch. Not a b!tch to forget everything every time."

The silence in the room turned heavier.

Even the wind outside seemed to be still.

She stood again and slowly walked to the window, lifting the corner of the curtain to glance outside, her fingers drumming lightly on the frame.

"I knew you people would come," she said calmly.

"In fact, I made sure of it."

Sitaramaju's voice grew firm.

"What do you mean, made sure?"

She turned around, her expression unreadable.

"The path you took... the fish vendor... the board that said Vellugodu Reservoir, even your Contact Person outside pretending to be startled that he made pride that he had contacts in my Village-all of it. I arranged that. It wasn't just any coincidence."

She paused.

"The moment the girl went missing, the balance here shifted. And he stirred."

Her voice dropped just slightly, suddenly cold and distant.

"And when she stirs... fate brings the right players to the house."

Abhimanyu frowned.

"Who's she? Who are you talking about?"

Adhrika stepped closer now, her face half-lit by the oil lamp's flame, casting shadows across her cheekbones.

"You'll meet her soon enough," she whispered. *"But first, I need you to understand — you didn't just walk into my house. You walked into a story that began before you were born."*

She raised a hand, made a gentle twisting motion in the air, and the flame in the lamp flickered violently, dancing shadows along the old walls.

"Now," she said, her tone suddenly crisp. *"Tell me everything. Every single thing about the girl. Because if you want her back..."* She paused, locking eyes with Sitaramaju—

"You'll need to do something none of your men have ever done before. You'll need to descend."

Sitarama Raju leaned forward, his silhouette wavering against the amber glow of the oil lamp.

His voice, though steady, carried the weight of buried terror. *"It began in my MANSION"* he said, eyes fixed on a point far beyond the room.

Adhrika and Abhimanyu remained silent, their attention sharpened by the gravity in his tone.

"The girl... her disappearance isn't just some twisted coincidence," he continued. *"The Sadhu... he holds a clue. Something deep, ancient. Something no man dares to voice aloud."*

He exhaled, heavy and slow.

"I followed that clue. It led me here. But before I could cross the last threshold—"

He paused. His hand trembled faintly on the table.

"I collapsed. Right near the cemetery gate. And in that unconscious void..." His voice dropped to a whisper. *"I saw them. Visions. Flickering shadows. A crimson thread pulling me forward... her slippers... the girl's voice calling from beyond..."*

He looked up, eyes reflecting something that was both fear and revelation.

"Whatever this place is... It's no ordinary ground. Something waits. And it's tied to her, and to me."

He paused.

"We were inside a half-built structure. With a roof. First floor open without any walls at the Entrance. Just the raw skeleton of concrete and exposed bricks, except at the Entrance. But what stood there, what called to me, was a wooden door frame. Like it was waiting. It looked like this..."

Sitaramaju gestured with his hands, tracing the outline. The image resembled an elegant, vintage door frame, like the one in the photo they'd seen, but hollowed, with no actual doors or windows. Only the frame remained.

"It had side frames too... like windows. But there was no glass. No doors. Just emptiness."

"And across the top..." he continued, voice dropping to a whisper, *"...A long **Red Ribbon**. Thick. Dark. Like blood dried in sunlight. It was tied tightly between the top corners of the frame, stretched from node to node. And on the other side, my brother..."*

He glanced at Abhimanyu.

"You were already inside the frame. Examining the ribbon. Careful. Curious. But just as you were about to step out, something changed."

Adhrika narrowed her eyes.

"Changed how?"

Sitaramaju stared at the lamp's flame. Then:

"The space inside the frame started to shimmer. And from inside the hollow window frame, a visual bled through. Like oil spilled across water. And then... it opened."

He drew a circle in the air with his finger.

"A circular portal. A dimensional hole. Through it, I've seen her."

Adhrika's breath caught.

"Your daughter?"

Sitaramaju nodded.[YES]

"She was barefoot. But smiling. She looked... safe. She was in a moving car on a highway. Traffic all around. And beside her, driving the car... was a woman. I couldn't see her face properly. Just the silhouette."

"Then the woman turned. She looked directly at me, like she saw me. Across dimensions. Through time. Through magic. And she said..."

He swallowed.

"She warned me: Stop looking for your daughter. She is Safe Here."

The room fell deathly silent.

Sitaramaju's words hung in the air like smoke.

"It was her... I know it now. The woman in the car was **Tantri.***"*

Adhrika froze. Her face, once calm and unreadable, flickered with something raw.

Ancient.

Fear.

Her throat twitched. Without saying a word, she staggered toward a ceramic pot by the corner. She fumbled for a glass, her fingers trembling, and scooped water from it, drinking in heavy gulps.

Not a spell.

Not a charm.

Just... water. Like a mortal.

Even the village heads & servants watching her from a distance exchanged uncertain glances. For a moment, the mighty witch looked utterly human, haunted by a memory too dark to be spoken aloud.

She exhaled hard, the glass still in her hand. The name had pierced something deep inside her.

"So,"

she finally whispered, almost to herself,

"She's back... again."

The words felt like a curse.

Without another glance, she turned and marched out of the room, her long black robe trailing behind her. Her footsteps were sharp now, deliberate.

She pushed open a creaking wooden door - her library. A vast, dimly lit chamber lined with shelves that reached the ceiling, sagging under the weight of scrolls, parchments, and tomes.

She didn't hesitate.

She began pulling out books one after another, not the flamboyant grimoires gilded with gold, but the old ones. The forgotten ones. Written in dying dialects. Inked in blood and bound in bark. Her fingers moved feverishly, flipping pages, muttering under her breath.

"Tantri... Tantri... where are you?"

The dust clouded her eyes, but she didn't blink. Her mind raced.

She pulled down a thick volume wrapped in cobwebs. Cracked it open.

"She was erased..."

She pulled another, tore past brittle pages.

"They bound her to silence..."

And then, she found something.

Her breath hitched.

An etching - a sigil, carved in charcoal - shaped like an eye with a slit and two wings branching from it. Beside it, a handwritten scrawl barely visible:

Tantri — The Disappeared Flame.

𖤐𖤐𖤐

Tantri — The Disappeared Flame.

Banished. Forgotten.

But never gone.

She whispered the final words aloud, barely audible:

"She was never meant to return..."

Adhrika's fingers slid across the old leather-bound book as if she'd done it a hundred times before. Its pages crackled with age, the ink faded in places, but still powerful, etched in a language lost to most, save for those who practiced the forgotten ways.

She flipped to the chapter marked with a blood-red thread.

The page read:

"She walks between veils. The one who claims daughters have not yet awakened. She does not seek death, nor ransom. She seeks transition-the moment before blood. The one thing all her victims share... is time.

She is the one who triggers the awakening — the first blood. The cycle begins not when the body chooses, but when she does."

Adhrika's lips pursed. Her voice dropped into a murmur, reading aloud:

"They vanish before the moon blesses their wombs. When innocence sleeps but womanhood stirs - she takes them. Not for sacrifice. Not for spite. But for balance, as twisted as it may be..."

As she finished, a suffocating silence fell in the room.

The flame in the corner sconce wavered. The oil pot beside her bubbled faintly. Everyone — from the servants to the remaining village heads - stood frozen. Eyes wide. Breaths shallow.

Then, breaking the silence, one of the village heads — an older man missing part of his scalp from a hunting accident, often referred to as **"Headless Naidu"** in village jest, staggered forward.

"I-I'll give her mine," he said suddenly, voice cracking with desperate emotion. *"Take my blood. Just... give back the girl. Take mine instead."*

For a moment, nobody moved.

Adhrika blinked.

Then she slowly turned her head toward him, eyes unreadable, a strange mix of pity and amusement crossing her face. She raised one brow and replied, with carefully restrained sarcasm:

"...First blood is not the first blood you think, You poor, deluded Naidu."

He tilted his head, confused. *"Eh?"*

"It's not a wound," she continued coldly. *"It's not a vein, or a knife, or a noble sacrifice. It's a girl's body... changing. Maturing. Becoming capable of bearing life."*

She closed the book with a soft thud.

"It's Menstruation, Naiduu.. **The first time a girl bleeds — not from pain, but from nature."**

A beat of silence. And then, as realization sank in the old man turned crimson, eyes falling to the floor. Slowly, he shuffled back, head hung low in mortified silence.

The servants dared not breathe.

Sitaramaju's fists tightened at his sides. *"So you mean to say... she only takes those about to enter womanhood?"*

Adhrika nodded grimly.

"She doesn't steal them. She waits. Like a predator. Or perhaps... like a midwife of the old world. One who believes she's doing them a favor. Saving them - before the world ruins them."

Abhimanyu's face darkened. *"Then she took our girl... just before her time."*

Adhrika looked at him, the shadows of her past flickering across her gaze.

"No," she said quietly. *"She took her… because of her time."*

Sitaramaraju slammed his fist against the wooden arm of his chair, the echo loud in the old stone chamber. His face was flushed with anger and despair.

"No girl has ever disappeared like this since I was born!" he roared. *"Not like this! Not from my house!"*

Adhrika placed a steadying hand on the table, her voice trembling with empathy.

"I understand your pain… and the guilt that burns in your chest like coal. But this isn't just any enemy, Sitaramaraju. This is Tantri."

She paused, her voice dropping as the shadows in the room seemed to lean in closer.

"Tantri was my Sister"

[Everyone paused for a moment]

"She was born long before I was… and practically raised me in the craft. She and my mother were the ones who taught me Earth-bound magic. But Tantri… she's not bound to Earth anymore. Not since she died. She's tethered to the world after death and from there, she draws power I can't even touch."

Abhimanyu stepped forward, the flame of the oil lamp catching his thoughtful eyes.

"Does your daughter know this magic?"

Adhrika fell silent. Her eyes sank to the floor.

"No," she whispered. *"My daughter died… in a fire accident."*

The room stilled.

"We had come to London to visit my granddaughter, who was studying there. That fire… it wasn't just a tragedy. It was the price of protecting her. The girl you saw… she's not my daughter. She's my granddaughter."

Abhimanyu's mind whirred.

"So… if your granddaughter and you were together once… could your combined strength be enough to challenge Tantri now?"

Adhrika turned her head slowly, a flicker of realization dawning. She walked to the far side of the room, toward a thick, leather-bound tome already open on its stand. The pages smelled of age and incense.

She flipped it once, twice, then stopped.

Her voice cut the air, clear and certain:

"Yes. It's possible."

The air shifted.

"I can't cross into other dimensions. I can't face Tantri in the after-death realm. But I channel my power — all of it, to my granddaughter."

She placed a hand on the page, her fingers trembling as they hovered over an ancient script.

"There's a law. A silent one, written in the oldest coven texts… If a witch dies in a natural disaster, her powers are automatically transferred to the next bloodline, but only on the child's 21st birthday."

Adhrika turned to face them, her eyes gleaming.

"Tara is just 20."

"In ten days, her 21st birthday arrives."

A long breath filled the room. The walls seemed to listen.

"With her mother's powers already inside her… and mine soon to be passed on… Tara will carry a triad flame strong enough to stand before Tantri. She won't need to run."

"She can fight."

Adhrika's eyes held the weight of secrets as the conversation lingered. "She can fight," she had declared, her voice low and resolute.

Without another word, Adhrika and Abhimanyu slipped quietly from the room, leaving the others behind. They made their way through a narrow corridor toward a familiar space, the very room where Tara had once greeted everyone with a bright, hopeful smile.

Outside, in the cool morning air, Tara remained with the old man, who was still trying to rouse some sense of awareness from his slumber. Her gentle presence amid the lingering mist lent an almost unreal calm to the chaos of the moment.

As they reached a quieter corner of the mansion, Abhimanyu, hope and concern mingling in his eyes, turned to Adhrika. Clasping his arms tightly to his body, he asked, voice steady despite the turmoil inside,

"What else is there for us to know about Tantri, and what is our plan now?"

Adhrika hesitated, a flicker of sorrow crossing her face, before she spoke in a low, sombre tone.

"My sister, Tantri—she was born on a New Moon, the night of no moonlight, swallowed by darkness."

She said slowly.

"That day, she held power beyond measure, more than I could ever claim."

She paused, memories swirling in her eyes as she continued,

"When she was just fifteen, she came crawling to my home from somewhere in the village. She was ill, her clothes in tatters... and she told me what had happened. But... I've forgotten so much with time."

Her voice trailed off, heavy with regret and loss, while Abhimanyu's face remained etched with both determination and sorrow. In that quiet moment, the echoes of the past and the uncertain promise of the future intertwined, A promise they would soon chase down the darkened trail toward Vellugodu.

"Wait... you said you don't remember?" he asked slowly, watching her every expression.

"But you're a witch. Aren't you supposed to remember everything... especially something like that?"

Adhrika didn't flinch. Her eyes, calm but unreadable, turned to him.

"I wasn't even born when she first came to our home," she said softly, a distant weight behind the words.

"What I know is only what she told me. And whatever she said... I couldn't hold on to all of it. Maybe she made me forget. Maybe I chose to."

Abhimanyu blinked. For the first time in days, doubt crept into his heart. He didn't show it outright, but inside, something cracked.

She had saved him. She had answered questions before he asked. She offered help when no one else did. And yet... There was a haze to her truths. A hesitation. A missing piece.

Why?(he asked himself)

Why now? Why him?

Adhrika turned away, walking slowly, her back to him.

He stood still.

And in that quiet moment...

He didn't know if she was shielding him from danger,

Or from the truth.

Abhimanyu followed Adhrika in silence, his thoughts still tangled. She led him to the old well where the old man stood, quiet and motionless, as though time itself had frozen around him.

"Go now," Adhrika said gently but firmly to the old man. *"Come back tonight. We have work to do."*

The old man nodded and slowly walked away without a word, disappearing into the twilight like a memory fading from sight.

Adhrika turned, her robes catching the light breeze, and faced Tara, who had just arrived, a curious expression on her face.

"Pack your things, Tara," she said casually, almost playfully. *"We leave tomorrow morning. We have a friend to visit in Kurnool."*

Tara tilted her head, a flicker of confusion turning into a smile.

"Is it a one-day trip?" she asked, her tone full of innocent excitement.

Adhrika's voice softened with an almost motherly warmth.

"No, dear. This time it's a month-long journey. There are... people we need to deal with." She smiled gently. *"And I've planned a surprise for your twenty-first birthday."*

Abhimanyu stood at a distance, watching, silently. Something inside him sank. Tara was radiant, glowing with the idea of travel, adventure, and the hint of a birthday surprise. But she had no idea what was waiting for her. She was still untouched by the weight of truth. Still protected.

And in that moment, as she turned and skipped off with joy to pack her things, her happiness lit the air around her like sunshine breaking through shadows. She smiled, wide and pure, like an angel. And as she tucked her hair behind her ear, eyes gleaming with anticipation, something in Abhimanyu's heart ached.

She didn't know.

Not yet.

And the world around her... was about to change forever.

As Tara disappeared into the house, humming a tune of her own joy, Adhrika turned slowly to Abhimanyu. Her expression, which had been soft just a moment ago, was now unreadable, somewhere between commanding and pleading.

"Tell everyone," she said firmly, her voice low. *"Tara must not know any of what we discussed. Not yet. I'll tell her… when the time comes."*

Abhimanyu nodded hesitantly, the weight of her request sinking in. There was more fear in his silence than in his words. Not fear of the plan, but fear of what lay ahead for the girl who still smiled like the world was untouched.

ϷϷϷ

Tara moved quietly around her room, folding her clothes with a lightness that almost made the night feel softer. Her briefcase lay open on the wooden bed, half-filled with neatly stacked fabrics. Every motion she made carried a sense of excitement, an innocence wrapped in charm.

Abhimanyu appeared at the doorway, unnoticed at first. He leaned casually against the wooden frame, one leg crossed over the other, his arms folded across his chest. His gaze lingered, caught between wonder and a silent dilemma. He still remembered the first time he had seen her through the window. When she had gently adjusted the curls falling across her face, tucking them behind her left ear with her left hand. That memory lingered within him, her smile replaying endlessly, as though eternity itself had folded into the present.

Finally, he broke the silence.

"Do you know where you're going?" His tone carried a hint of suspicion, but also curiosity.

Tara glanced at him, her eyes bright, lips curving with mischief.

"I don't know," she admitted softly, *"but I do know that it will be fun. Anything outside this mansion will be better."*

Abhimanyu studied her, a faint smile flickering. Then he said, his voice steady,

"Well... I'll show you a special place when we reach my hometown."

Her face lit up instantly. The spark in her eyes was almost childlike, brimming with thrill. She leaned in slightly, as if the world had just whispered her a secret.

"Tell me what it is," she pressed eagerly.

Abhimanyu chuckled, shaking his head. "A surprise is meant to be surprised... not to be suppressed."

She narrowed her eyes playfully.

"Fine... then we have a deal. To claim this surprise, I'll cook a special dinner tonight. Only for you. And yes, it's a surprise dish."

His smile deepened. *"Then it's settled."*

The tension softened, and instead of drifting into an embrace, they extended their hands. Their fingers met in a firm yet tender handshake, an unspoken promise hanging quietly between them.

ｷｷｷ

That night, under the moonlit sky, dinner was arranged near the ancient well. A wooden table stood by the stone edge, plates scattered, laughter spilling softly as some leaned against the mossy walls, and others sat cross-legged on the ground. The British-era mansion loomed in the background, its shadow watching over them like a quiet guardian of time.

Abhimanyu sat in his guest room apart; he heard the soft creak of wheels break the silence. Tara entered, pushing a trolley, arranged with care, just like in fine restaurants. She stopped before him, her voice playful yet gentle.

"May I come, Abhi?"

The word struck him still. He looked up, stunned. *"Abhi?"* he repeated slowly.

"No one has called me that in ages... but,"

[he paused]

He rubbed his palms together nervously, then let a faint smile rise & said,

"It's sweet when you say it. Come in."

He leaned back, watching her with curiosity. *"So tell me... what special dish did you make for me?"* His voice carried rare excitement.

Tara grinned, placing a plate before him. *"Not so fast. At least give me one glimpse of the surprise you promised me, no?"*

He hesitated, glancing at her innocent face, then gave in with a chuckle. *"Alright. It's a place where you'll be surrounded by water on all four sides... but it's not an ocean. That's all I can say."*

She served the food gracefully, sliding the plate toward him. He tasted it and froze. His eyes glistened. *"This...*

This tastes like my granny's cooking." His voice cracked, and before she could answer, she pulled her gently into a side hug, brushing his shoulder. *"You've given me more than food tonight...*

You gave me Memory."

She smiled softly, resting her hand on his arm for a moment, then let him eat in peace. When he finished, he whispered, *"Thank you, Tara."*

As she turned to leave, she looked back, her eyes playful. *"Can I know just one more hint about the place?"*

This time, he didn't hesitate. A boyish charm flickered on his face. *"It's called Dolphin. Now go—sleep. No more questions until tomorrow."*

She laughed under her breath and left the room, her presence lingering. Soon after, the night deepened, and one by one, the mansion and its people drifted into silence, the old walls keeping watch.

The Illusion

<u>The Sleeping Walls</u> :

A few hours before sunrise, the British mansion lay wrapped in an uneasy stillness. Inside, bodies lay scattered across floors and beds in deep slumber, weary from the strange day behind them and unaware of what the coming dawn would demand.

Outside, at the gate, a handful of servants had been tasked with the night watch. A fire flickered weakly in the iron brazier beside them, casting long shadows against the ancient walls. One servant leaned back on a wooden chair, arms folded, breath slowing, then finally giving in to sleep. Another sat propped against a stone pillar, head bobbing before it, too, surrendered.

The night was still. But not silent.

Somewhere from the dense thicket near the edge of the estate grounds came a subtle crack—like a dry branch splitting under pressure. A moment passed.

Then another.

A wind that didn't belong in the world of nature stirred the leaves. It didn't move the trees, but it did whisper.

From that single oil lantern - hanging from the edge of the third-floor rooftop - drops of oil began to fall, slow and steady, like time itself was leaking. Minutes passed. The wind, which had been blowing eastward all night, suddenly shifted to the north, carrying the scent of something ancient... and alert.

The drops, carried now by the redirected wind, curved midair and landed directly on the flame-lit torch—A traditional one made of resin-soaked cloth wrapped tightly around a stick, placed to light the outer grounds of the mansion. With each drop that struck the torch's core, the flame hissed and grew, swelling in size with a sly, sinister smirk.

Within seconds, the torch blazed brighter, flaring unnaturally-its shadow stretching long and fierce against the west wing of the mansion.

No one stirred.

Except one.

Abhimanyu.

The man who had once faced fire and walked through it. The man whose name echoed a warrior's spirit.

He lay inside, asleep on a cotton bed, wearing a plain white cut-sleeve banyan. But something in the subtle crackling and the rise of heat through the wall itched at his senses.

He flinched. His brow furrowed.

Eyes opened slowly. Not in fear, but in curiosity... concern.

He sat up, bracing his arms on either side of the bed. The flickering light from outside painted wavering shadows across his muscular back, almost like smoke was forming directly from his skin. His face turned to the right - toward the faint glow beyond the window.

The glass was hazy. Old. Not transparent.

He rose, walked slowly to it, and swung his left hand across the glass to wipe it clean.

The image became clear. The flame had grown.

Abhimanyu's eyes narrowed. Trained.

He gently unlatched the window and opened it. From this angle, he spotted the source—the oil dripping from the old lantern above. It was feeding the flame.

Without hesitation, he turned and made his way up to the third floor. Boots silent against the wooden stairs. His body calm, but his instincts alert.

He reached the rooftop edge and found the lantern.

Loose. Tilted. Its old brass cap barely holding.

He adjusted it, tightening the nod, and wiping off the excess oil that had overflowed.

And that's when he saw it.

His gaze drifted to the distant driveway, and there, parked with silent pride, was a silver open-top car—low-slung, metallic, elegant, like it didn't belong to this time.

It looked like a beast crafted for the wind. The silver body was polished to perfection, almost glowing under the flickering torchlight. The contours were fluid—as if carved by motion itself. Twin circular headlamps glowed steadily, not harsh but persistent. The rear lights were on too, soft like coals—almost pulsing.

The interior, from what he could make out even at that height, gleamed with deep red leather. Wooden trim. A large manual gear lever. A dashboard of dials and chrome. The kind of car that didn't just move—it spoke, even when silent.

It was powered, he could tell, by an inline-six engine, judging by the length of the hood and symmetry of the body. The kind of engine that purred when idle but could growl when provoked.

He blinked. It wasn't there before.

And yet...

It felt like it belonged.

He descended again. Past the sleeping halls. Past the front corridor.

Out the main doors.

The cold night air hit him first, but his focus never wavered. The servants stationed as watchmen at the gate? Slumped in sleep like corpses. Not even the swelling torchlight had woken them.

Abhimanyu walked past them with a faint laugh under his breath. *"Hell of a watch,"* he muttered.

He stepped forward, toward the car.

The silver ghost sat still.

He circled around, observing it. No footsteps. No signs of arrival. No tire imprints. No engine sound. And yet the engine felt warm, as though it had just been turned off.

He moved closer. The leather on the driver's side seat looked sunken slightly, as if someone had only just gotten out.

He stood still. Staring at it.

As though it was staring back.

He stood there.

Staring.

Ten minutes... maybe more.

The wind had stilled. The flames behind him flickered gently, casting long shadows that slowly stretched and then curled back like they were breathing.

But he didn't blink.

That silver open-top car remained still, poised like a sculpture. Not a single soul around. No footsteps. No sounds of approach. No breeze. Nothing.

And yet — the keys were still in the ignition.

The engine was on.

Not loud. No roar. Just a low, warm hum... like the car was purring, waiting.

Abhimanyu's brows drew slightly together. A muscle in his jaw tensed. He stepped forward — boots crunching softly on the stone path, the sound swallowed by the cold stillness of the night.

What's it doing here?
Who drove it?

Why is no one inside…?

His eyes drifted over its form again. The silver body, smooth as mercury under the torchlight, carried a timelessness… something older than chrome or horsepower. The leather seats glistened as if untouched by dust. The dashboard lights glowed in soft amber, giving life to the car's chest.

He felt something rise within him, not fear. But curiosity laced with awe.

His eyes, once drawn to the vehicle's shape, now caught something else, the reflection.

In the smooth curve of the windshield, he saw not just himself, but behind him — the towering shadow of the mansion, the flames still glowing, and… something faint in the sky.

The London skyline.

He blinked.

The cobbled road under the car, the gentle curve of the pavement, the way the faint light danced along the stone… wasn't that… Piccadilly side? Kensington corner? That sharp cross turn?

It was London.

But he was still in India. In the hills. In the shadows of an old temple mansion.

And yet, he was staring at London's roads, reflecting from a car that didn't belong here… or perhaps belonged everywhere.

Abhimanyu looked around once more.

No footsteps.

No sound.

Not a soul stirred.

Only the hum of the engine… and a strange calmness in his chest.

As if the car had arrived not from a road...

...but from a memory.

Or a warning.

Or a dream.

And still, no one came forward.

So he stood there.

Staring. Admiring. Wondering.

"Why are you here?" he finally whispered. Not to himself.

But to the car.

And for a moment...

he thought it might answer.

Abhimanyu exhaled slowly.

He glanced once more toward the sleeping mansion, then back at the car — as though expecting someone to yell his name... or for the dream to collapse.

But nothing changed.

The engine still hummed.

The leather interior still glistened.

So, he took a final step forward — and laid his hand gently on the edge of the driver's door.

Click.

The door unlatched without resistance, smooth as if freshly tuned. Not a squeak. Not a groan.

He opened it.

A gentle warmth wafted out from the inside, not like heat from a fire, but something more subtle... more human. The scent of aged leather, burnt coffee, and something faintly metallic — like rain on iron.

He slid in.

The seat embraced him softly, fitting as if it remembered his weight.

His fingers hovered over the steering wheel. The wood-textured rim felt cold — unnaturally cold for an engine that had clearly been running for a while.

He didn't turn the wheel.

He didn't press the pedal.

Not yet.

His eyes moved across the dashboard. Everything was intact. Analog dials... glowing softly. Speedometer stuck at zero, but the tachometer flickered slightly — alive.

Then he noticed something.

The glove compartment... was slightly ajar.

Abhimanyu reached out.

His fingers brushed the edge, and the small door eased open with a soft creak. Inside — a crisp envelope, a tool kit, and a few chocolates. No dust, no wear — like they had just been placed there minutes ago.

He picked it up.

In bold, handwritten ink:

"ENJOY YOU'RE RIDE"

He frowned. The odd grammar didn't bother him as much as the feeling it gave — like a whisper from something ancient trying to sound... friendly.

He said it aloud, almost jokingly:

"Enjoy you're ride?"

Click. Snap. THWUMP.

Without warning — the car reacted.

The seat belt shot across his chest like a whip. Another wrapped tightly over his right shoulder, then left, then his neck — gently but firmly, like a serpent coiling with purpose. At the same moment, a sleek, metallic sheet began sliding out from the trunk, arching upward and forward with mechanical grace. The open-top car was no longer open — the roof sealed shut above him, cutting off the night air, as if enclosing him inside a decision that could not be undone.

He gasped — but it wasn't pain. It was containment.

The belt secured him not just across the chest, but over his upper arms, torso, and just stopped at the thighs — like the machine knew exactly what to control and what to leave free.

Then the engine roared.

Not loud... but alive.

The car lurched forward, turning by itself, tires whispering against the stone road as it navigated silently out of the mansion gate — past the sleeping servants, past the flickering torch, past the heavy wooden entrance.

He didn't touch the wheel.

He didn't need to.

The road bent. The car followed.

Faster... and faster.

The old British trees vanished into a blur. Fields rolled past in waves. The sky was still dark, but the horizon had begun to bleed orange, just a hint — like a secret being revealed in slow motion.

They drove.

And drove.

Until finally, the car slowed... as if it had arrived.

Ahead, a range of mountains towered in silhouette. But one stood out: jagged, black, and sharp against the rising blue, with a red-glowing fissure slicing through its side — not lava... but something else. Something pulsing.

And just at the base of the mountain:

An abandoned railway track. A rusted train engine frozen mid-turn. And near it... a giant stone gate with ancient carvings glowing faintly.

The car stopped.

Abhimanyu couldn't move. He could only stare.

Then, faintly...

The dashboard radio turned on by itself.

A woman's voice.

Soft. Unfamiliar.

"Now that we've arrived... she will remember you."

Along the way... a train came.

Not on the tracks behind the mansion — but cutting through the edge of the mountains ahead. Steam billowed from its chimney, hissing into the cold air like a sigh of something long buried.

Abhimanyu turned his head, watching it — mesmerized.

The train's metallic body was worn but majestic. The kind of train you'd expect in sepia-tinted photographs — too old to still exist, too new to be history.

As it thundered nearer, his instincts kicked in.

He jerked the handle, tried to kick open the door, but it wouldn't budge.

Suddenly — a flicker in his mind.

A tool kit.

Lying in the dashboard tray beside the faded envelope and chocolates.

His fingers wrapped around it.

Moments before, he had opened the toolkit — old, locked, yet untouched for years. But inside, the tools lay still, silent, and shining. No dust, no rust — it was clean as people in Heaven.

And there it was — a screwdriver, resting perfectly in place like it had been waiting just for him.

He held it tightly, staring. Something in him whispered:

Try it. Wake up.

With resolve, he stabbed the tip of the screw driver into his left bicep.

No blood. No pain

Nothing.

That's when he realized —

This wasn't real. Or at least, not the kind of real he knew.

He blinked.

And like a fog being cleared, the radio fuzz vanished. The whispering voice died. The cabin grew cold.

He unscrewed the screwdriver, broke it into pieces, and used a sharp metal piece to slide into the door's safety lock groove.

Click.

The door eased open — not forcefully, but like it had just been waiting for him to know.

But the moment his foot touched the ground—

The World Shifted.

No longer by the glowing fissure.

No train. No stone gate.

Now, he was driving.

Not in control of the car exactly... but not being restrained either. The seatbelt was back — but loose, protective. Not imprisoning.

And he was on a mountain valley road.

It spiralled like a ribbon around the cliffs. The sky was a violet blend of night fading into dawn.

Abhimanyu, dressed in a crisp white shirt with half-folded sleeves and dark blue denim jeans, steps into a silver-colored convertible. The car's sleek dashboard is black, the seats upholstered in a rich cream shade. With only two door handle nobs, the vehicle exudes both elegance and power as he settles into the open-top ride.

As the car moved along a black tar road, marked with solid white border lines and dashed lines in the center, the red tail lights glowed softly. Coming down from the

mountain road, Abhimanyu turned his head to the left &
Right, gazing thoughtfully at the sweeping valley view
below."

Below him, in the vast distance:

To his Left

The once-thriving city lay in ruins, its towering
structures engulfed in fire. Skyscrapers cracked and
crumbled as black flames erupted from their cores, rising
like monstrous clouds against the scorched sky.

Streets that once bustled with life now echoed with
silence, broken only by the distant roar of collapsing
buildings. Birds flew in frantic flocks, many caught in the
blaze, their burning wings streaking across the smoke-filled
air. Entire blocks were ablaze—rooftops glowing red,
windows shattering from the heat—while dark smoke
billowed upward, drowning the skyline in a storm of ash
and sorrow.

To his Right

The small village had become a graveyard of memories.
Children had once run through the fields with cows, and
a distant temple bell rang like a heartbeat through calm
mornings.

Now, homes were set on fire—roofs collapsing, flames
devouring everything once known and loved. Villagers,
chained and dragged into labor lines, stumbled barefoot
over scorched earth, their eyes hollow, their spirits fading.
Some collapsed on the blackened road—barely breathing,
but still alive—while smoke coiled around them like a cruel
reminder of everything they had lost.

Abhimanyu held the wheel — but the car seemed to
know the road better than he did.

He wasn't sure what was real anymore.

But this place... felt like a memory.

Or maybe a warning.

As the car glided along the winding mountain path, Abhimanyu began to notice something strange.

The road beneath him... started to vanish.

Not instantly, but fading like ink dissolving in water.

There was no bump, no crash, no jolt.

Just a slight tilt, a quiet lift.

And suddenly... the car seat detached .

Not from the ground, but from gravity itself.

Abhimanyu felt it.

That cold whisper of air around his ankles.

The wheels no longer touched anything.

He looked around — his car seat was rising, gently, like it had become part of a balloon, carried upward into the misted sky.

He gasped and gripped the arms of the seat.

Below him, the road curved away, then disappeared entirely — swallowed by clouds and thin air.

He looked back at the car, now dangling, still connected to him by something fluttering in the air.

It was a RIBBON.

A single, dark **RED RIBBON**

Flowing like silk in the wind, tied loosely between the back of his seat and the car.

The ribbon stretched.

And stretched.

Further... and further.

The distance between him and the car grew — yet the ribbon held, as if resisting the separation.

It shimmered under the morning sun, red, but not blood red. Something older, deeper.

The kind of red that felt like it had a story.

Abhimanyu's heart raced.

He wasn't falling.

He was ascending.

He looked up.

Through the golden haze above, he could see an old lady—her form flickering like smoke—trying to speak.

Her lips trembled as her eyes locked onto his.

"FINALLY… YOU ARE HERE, ABHI!!," she whispered.

Abhimanyu's eyes widened. He drew a sharp breath, his body frozen, caught between awe and disbelief.

His chest heaved. His hands clenched.

The music swelled—rising drums pounding like a heartbeat, layered with a resonant hum—as she floated closer.

Then, with a gentle, eerie smile, she added:

"WELCOME. TO. MY. WORLD."

The light dimmed. The air grew colder.

And Abhimanyu knew—he had crossed into something far beyond his understanding.

THE ILLUSION

THE ILLUSION

www.ingramcontent.com/pod-product-compliance
Lightning Source LLC
Chambersburg PA
CBHW041334120726
48005CB00014B/2246